METRO CITY

A Metro City Novel

KATRINA AVANT

Katrina'sWorks

PUBLISHING LLC

Katrina'sWorks
Publishing, LLC

ISBN-13: 9780998218922

Metro City

Copyright © November 2018

Katrina Avant

K a t r i n a a v a n t - a u t h o r . c o m

Cover Design

Soul Sister Ink

K a t r i n a s w o r k s . c o m

METRO CITY

Prologue

Like the repeat of an over done movie scene, Eric Valero, cradling his new wife in his arms, franticly shouted for someone to help them. KT was barely breathing with a growing puddle of blood pooling around them. He tried stopping the life draining flow by pressing the wound with the palms of his trembling hands, but it continued to pour past the minute crevices between his fingers despite his efforts.

"Please! Somebody please help us!" He was on the verge of panic as he tried repositioning her; hoping this new angle would miraculously halt the blood flow. KT stared up at the sky, as if she was unaware of the mayhem erupting around them or the fact that she had been shot. Justin Graham, Eric's best man and best friend, was doing his best to shelter the couple from the stampeding crowd looking to escape the rapidly fired bullets.

After being announced husband and wife, Eric and KT stood hand in hand before their guests with pure joy. But the moment was short lived with the sudden sound of the first bullets ripping through the air. When the shots rang out, Eric instinctively grabbed the collapsing KT; bring them both down onto the perfectly manicured lawn. It was once they landed that he discovered she had been hit. It was now that he stared at the impossibly green turf, as if it held all the answers to the ensuing madness that threatened to trample them.

Feeling more blood exiting the wound, Eric drew a sharp unsteady breath at the widening stain collecting on his bride's otherwise pristine off white, crystal beaded dress. Disbelievingly, he watched her eyes flutter close as she lost consciousness. He closed his own eyes; praying it was all a dream that would end once he opened them. He thought it had to be some obscene joke that was being played out beyond the punch line. There was no way his lovely KT was lying on the ground dying.

Eric was slowly losing touch with everything that was going on around him. His mind, refusing to comprehend it all, chose to shut out the chaos and instead turn inward, in search of serenity. He couldn't even hear the screams of the guests who were scrambling to take cover. More blood gushed forth while he desperately tried to make it all go away. Someone stumbled over his foot; dislodging his highly polished loafer. The shoe landed on its side as the panicked guest righted himself before falling on top of the couple. The clumsy kick reminded Eric they were still in crisis mode and that he couldn't afford to check out from the pandemonium.

Reclaiming his slipping mind, Eric parted his lips to be heard over the deafening commotion. But before he could shout out a third time, Jon and Landon Payne were at his side, with Jon hurriedly removing his jacket and rolling up the sleeves of his dress shirt. The brothers had to forcefully maneuver through the throngs of people who were trying to escape the sniper's madness. And although the gunman's rampage had seemingly ceased, the crowd wasn't taking any chances that the shooting wouldn't start up again. They wanted to be as far away from the open air scene as possible.

Wide-eyed, Eric anxiously pleaded with Jon. "You have to help her!"

Despite the fact that Jon was trying to release his hold on her, Eric continued to possessively cling to KT. Now that someone was actually there to help, Eric had allowed himself to move further into shock. So focused on his dying wife, he didn't realize he was hindering Jon from helping her.

While Jon continued his tug of war with Eric, Landon joined Justin in blocking the trio from the slacking stream of fleeing guests. Most had either vacated the garden or was hugging the ground for safety. Grabbing the arm of a passing coworker, Landon took charge; bellowing at the woman and those of his colleagues in shouting distance, to lock the place down. They needed to find the culprit or culprits before they fled the grounds. With this task completed, he knelt at Jon's side to see what he could do to help.

Nodding towards Eric, Jon instructed his brother, "Help me get her flat on the ground!" He needed Landon to get Eric to comprehend he was there to help and back off. Landon nodded his understanding. He quickly maneuvered around him to attend to Eric.

"Eric, we're here. Let us help her." Landon gentle pried Eric's fingers from KT's body, so Justin could help Jon lay her flat. Sensing Eric wanted to reclaim his protectiveness of his wife, Landon grabbed him and held firmly to his shoulders so his brother could address KT's injury, just as Shelby Kirkland brought Jon's medical bag from the car.

Kneeling, Shelby adjusted her own attire; smoothly transitioning into triage nurse, while Jon ripped open the bodice of KT's wedding gown in search of the damage. She had been hit in her left side. Jon used a wad of Shelby's fore-offered gauze to clean away enough blood to assess the wound. After taking in the extent of the injury, he and Shelby exchanged their concerns. It didn't look good. They needed to get her to the hospital immediately!

"Where the hell are the paramedics?!" This time it was Dr. Payne who shouted.

Chapter 1

Eric Valero admired his reflection in the tuxedo shop's ornate, tri-fold mirror that stood in the center of the dressing area. Never one for this sort of attire, he had to admit; he looked damn good in the perfectly tailored suit. He was having his final fitting before the wedding and it couldn't have come at a better time. Not only was he marrying his fiancé, private investigator Kaitlin "KT" Ellis, but he had been promoted in rank to lieutenant with the Metro City Police Department. The brass thought it was high time to reward him for the good work he was doing within his division. But the greatest promotion would come later. At the end of the week, he would become husband of Mrs. Kaitlin Tamara Valero and he couldn't be more ready.

After the engagement, they decided to hold off on wedding plans until the city's latest unrest had died down. With two murder cases, the newest scandal concerning yet another city official and Dr. Guyton going off the rails, his division had a lot on its plate. But once the lull settled in, they wasted no time in planning a simple but elegant ceremony.

Outside of a few minor mishaps here and there, Metro City was quiet for once and he was grateful for the reprieve. It was time for a slice of happiness. The only shadow that stood cold over his joy was the unsolved murder of Alonso Kane and the shooting of his newest detective, Landon Payne. Although they suspected the two to be related, try as they could, he and Landon weren't able to solve the puzzle. After shooting Landon, all traces of the perpetrator seem to just vanish altogether. If it weren't for a real death and real bullets fired at them that day, he would have thought the unknown assailant truly was an apparition. Apart from that and the respite in crime, the only activity that rivaled the preparation for their special day was the city's mayoral race.

With crime down considerably, every candidate used the low stats as a promise to continue the trend once he or she gained office. Metro City's citizens, still punch drunk from all the recent scandals, were anxious to see those promises kept. Even though the credit was attributed to the current mayor, it was a surprise to everyone when she announced she wouldn't be running; citing she only took on the task because of Craven Wallace's conviction and incarceration. She was more than happy to be returning to her formerly quiet and simple life. Most of the citizens thought she was doing an excellent job and had settled in to elect her to the position permanently.

The two top contenders, Alec Campbell and Ryan Hamilton, were running neck and neck in the race for the coveted seat. Both, fairly newcomers to this particular political arena, appeared more than capable of taking on the job. Alec Campbell's only edge over his opponent was his previous citizenship before returning to Metro City, after moving away during his childhood. Campbell's rival, Ryan Hamilton, who was a long standing Metro City transplant, was impressively gaining traction in proving his worth over the native born son.

"Well old man, I see from that smile you're ready for the lock down," Justin Graham teased his friend. He was to be Eric's best man. They became friends years ago, after Justin launched his security company, Graham Security Inc.

"Man," Eric shook his head, "Who would have thought meeting KT at your house that night would have brought us to this point?" Eric met Kaitlin Ellis while she was serving as Justin's bodyguard, at a time Justin would like to forget.

Justin grinned. "You two are the perfect couple. I'm happy for you man." Justin embraced Eric with a pound to the back.

Eric turned from the embrace to admire his image once more in the antique mirror before removing his jacket at the attendant's request. "How are things going with you and Virginia?" Virginia was Justin's girlfriend and former nanny to his daughter.

Uncomfortable with the change of subject, Justin absent-mindedly squeezed the back of his neck before shaking his head. "She just got back from helping her mother get on her feet after a hip replacement." Justin's answer was hesitant and short. He really didn't know what to say beyond that; so in place of words, he gave Eric an apathetic shrug.

Virginia had been away awhile, but once she returned, he had somehow become apprehensive and guarded whenever their relationship was mentioned. They had been together since he gained sole custody of his daughter Cara, after his former wife went to prison.

Handing the perfectly cut jacket back to the boutique's elderly tailor, Eric frowned. He was surprised at his friend's side stepping the question. He wanted Justin to be as happy as he was.

"You don't sound too happy that she's back. What's going on with you two?"

Justin shrugged again. "I don't know. Something's off with us. I like her, I like her a lot, but I don't know if I want to be married again and that's what she wants. I really can't blame her. She deserves that, but I don't know if I'm the one to give it to her." After enduring a hellacious marriage to his ex-wife, he had all but trashed the institution.

Eric didn't like the sound of this. "You can't shy away because the last one didn't work out. And you and I both know it couldn't because you never should have married Anastasia in the first place." Eric was referring to Justin's farce of a marriage to wealthy socialite Anastasia Stanton who had manipulated him into the unholy union.

"I know, I know. But you also know Paige is the only woman I've ever loved and after I messed that up…" They both knew how and why that ended.

"The only real regret I have with the possibility of losing Virginia is Cara. She loves her. Virginia has been the only stable female in her life. It will break Cara's heart if we break up. And if we do break up, there is no way we can go back to being just employer and employee. Besides, Cara is in school now and doesn't need a full time nanny anymore. Virginia and I agreed that she should direct her time elsewhere, so I helped her find another job. She's even found another place to live. I won't cut Virginia out of my daughter's life because we didn't make it. She is a healthy, happy, well-adjusted little girl. It took us some time, but we're finally close like father and daughter should be and much of that is due to Virginia."

"Have you taken Cara to see her mother?" Eric knew it was a touchy subject. For a long time after Justin gained custody, Cara cried for her mother day and night, despite Virginia's presence. The little girl couldn't understand why her mother was suddenly no longer present in her life. Coupled with living with a father she barely knew was devastating.

Justin shook his head. "Anastasia won't allow it. She doesn't want Cara seeing her like that. In a way, she has a point; although Cara may grow to resent her for it when she's old enough to understand the circumstances of her mother's absence." Justin shrugged.

Justin told Cara her mother was on a secret adventure far away; a story concocted by Anastasia, who never wanted their daughter to know the truth. Justin played into the lie by reading Cara bedtime stories centered on extravagant characters and adventures. He assured Cara she would see her mother again whenever the stories weren't enough. Even as he told his daughter these half-truths, he hoped he was doing the right thing. He knew how a lie could cause irreparable damage. He was a living witness to its destruction.

"On the bright side, she sees her grandmother on a regular basis; now that she's moved to Metro City. After everything fell apart, there wasn't anything left for Mrs. Stanton in North Carolina. At least Cara has her maternal grandmother if she doesn't have her mother." Justin shrugged again. He had to accept whatever he could get when it came to his daughter's needs.

Eric was about to add more on the subject when his phone rang. He held up a finger; indicating he wanted to continue their discussion. As Eric listened to the caller, his expression grew grim. Justin knew that look. He was needed back at the precinct. He nodded his goodbye, as Eric headed back to the dressing room with the phone still pressed to his ear. They would have to continue their discussion another time. Eric was back on the clock.

Chapter 2

After not getting a desired answer, disturbed, Alec Campbell stared at the cheap disposable phone before tossing it back into a desk drawer. It had been weeks and he still hadn't heard from his associate. The man had followed orders perfectly, before straying off his appointed path and taking his own initiative, by taking shots at the police. After that, he suddenly dropped out of sight without warning.

Alec thought he would fall dead after hyperventilating over the news of the young detective Landon Payne being shot. He didn't have to wonder who the culprit was. It was his own fault for telling the man of his underhanded deeds. But he had to be cocky; boasting about how he was the one who orchestrated the latest scandal that ruined so many lives, including his associate's. Had he known the man would react the way he had, Alec would have kept that tidbit of information to himself; at least until after the man had finished his assigned tasks.

Deep in thought, Alec pulled at his chin. It was much too late to rethink that debacle. The compulsive idiot's absence continued to worry him. He had become more than unpredictable; he had become a liability; a ticking bomb waiting to go off God knows when or where. This was something he could not afford if he was to become Metro City's next mayor. He had worked too hard and been too careful for things to fall apart now. Alec began to regret even hiring the man. He should have scrutinized his choice more closely, but he thought the younger man was hungry enough to be controlled. Now he was the one who was paying the price. That was his mistake; a mistake he wouldn't be making a second time.

Pulling the phone from its hiding place once more, he punched in some numbers to make a second call. His current subordinate may be missing, but he still had tasks that needed tending to. He reluctantly would have to resort to plan B. He may have an edge over his opponent in the mayoral race for now; but if things weren't handled and handled with caution, he could kiss that position goodbye. He wasn't too worried about any other consequences. He was certain he covered his tracks well enough not to be tied to the fool if he were caught.

∞

Alec's plan B paced around the piss stained holding cell; berating himself for being so careless as to get caught in the act. But he was in a hurry to get the shipment done so he could get to the job he coveted the most; the job *he* should have had in the first place. The boss was willing to pay him a quarter of a million dollars to complete the task that deranged moron left unfinished. But now that he had been caught, that dream, along with the money, was down the drain. With what the cops caught him holding, he was sure to do some serious time if he didn't come up with a counter action to this mess. There was only one way he knew for sure that he didn't do much time, if any at all. He would have to tell everything he knew. At this point, freedom was more valuable than money. He was just wanted for drug trafficking not murder. With the current political climate, along with his racial ethnicity, the two crimes may as well be one and the same. But he still held hope for a better outcome. If he could make a *deal*, maybe the feds would look the other way and let him slide with the whole interstate drug running thing. What he knew could solve cases *and* put a couple of very important people away.

Plan B grinned wide at this prospect. He was so confident that he was about to make a deal of a life-time he stopped pacing to lie down on the cell's single, dingy cot; kicking up his feet, as a self-congratulatory pat on the back for his brilliant idea. He had to take care of himself. Whatever happens, he wasn't about to go down alone; especially since he was only a player and not the head of the operation. Alec Campbell may have been smart enough to not lay his hands on anything criminal, but he still knew where the so-called bodies were buried. Plan B grinned even wider.

∞

Landon Payne sat at his desk mindlessly rolling a pen back and forth across its cluttered surface. The Brooks Brothers fountain pen was a gift from his brother for making detective. In spite of having just made the bust of a lifetime, Alonso Kane's murder just wouldn't allow him to bask in the after-glow. He felt there was something simple he was missing about the unsolved case; something right in front of him, but he couldn't put his hands on it.

Finally tossing the pen in a drawer, he scratched at the stubble that started to grow on his cleft chin. Landon had completed a three day stake out and should have been home getting some much needed sleep, but he was too wired. Willie Boy Tucker, (aka Alec Campbell's Plan B), claimed he had information on the Kane case. But when pressed about it, he refused to say more unless he could make a deal.

"Where is he?" Eric asked, referring to Landon's catch of the day.

Landon was so deep in thought he hadn't realized Eric was standing over him until he spoke. Leaning back in his chair, he sighed before answering. He would have to put his obsession with Kane on hold for now. But if Willie Boy had some real information, just maybe he could solve this. He didn't hold out for much hope. He thought Willie Boy was grasping at straws to lighten his sentencing load.

"I placed him back in holding. He refuses to talk until he has an airtight deal in place."

"What kind of negotiation does he expect to have considering he was literally caught with a boat load of heroine marked for shipment to other states? The feds will want most of him with what he was moving."

Landon's team had arrested Willie Boy and his squad with more drugs than the department had ever seized. Craven Wallace and his crew hadn't even possessed that much. The group was caught on the secluded, low end of Belle River harbor loading the shipment unto an old rented freighter. It was the boat's owner who gave them the tip. The man felt something was off about Willie boy and his undisclosed purpose for the freighter.

Landon shrugged. "Whatever it is has him pretty confident." He strongly doubted Willie Boy could pull off a deal either.

Eric's jaw tightened. He hoped this wasn't another set up. The last person that promised the moon on this case, not only placed Landon's life in jeopardy, but ended up dead himself. He opened his mouth to address that very sentiment when pandemonium broke out in the squad room. Several of Eric's officers were scrambling towards prisoner lock up in a panic. Not liking this one bit, Landon and Eric both raced towards the growing commotion. They had to push their way through the crowd in order to reach the open cell. There was Willie Tucker convulsing on the floor with two uniformed officers trying to administer lifesaving measures to keep him alive. After a while, the seizures stopped with the suspect staring glassy eyed in their direction. One of the officers, working feverishly, pounded on the suspect's chest, but to no avail. The man was dead.

Landon hung his head and sighed in dismal defeat. "So much for any information coming from him," he mumbled. Throwing up his hands, he retraced his steps back to the squad room.

Staring at Willie Boys blank and seemingly accusing stare, Eric swiped a frustrated hand across his closely cropped hair. Every time it seemed they were getting close, someone died. He blinked, before giving the man's body a cursory sweep. There were no outward signs of foul play, but there was no doubt in his mind that the man lying lifeless on the grungy floor was murdered. But how?

∞

After exhausted measures were taken to revive the suspect, one of the officers who administered the prisoner's aid, got to his feet. But not before retrieving the empty water bottle he had given Willie Boy prior to the seizure. He shrugged apologetically at Eric, indicating he did his best. But unbeknownst to anyone there, he was the reason Willie Boy was dead. Clutching the bottle just behind his meaty right thigh, he didn't have to do much to conceal it. Everyone was so fixated on the now dead suspect, no one bothered to watch him leave the cell, let alone toss the evidence into the over flowing trash container just outside of Eric's office. And even if they had, anyone would have assumed it belonged to him. He was known to have a bottle or two on hand most of his shift. He had even been teased about it; with some of his fellow coworkers hinting that he may have had more than just water in those bottles. They all had a good laugh about it. But if they only knew.

Moments before the chaos, Sergeant Owen Meeks handed William "Willie Boy" Tucker a water bottle laced with cyanide. Meeks, the squad's lone mole planted by Alec Hamilton, was tying up loose ends. Willie, not suspecting Meeks was on Alec's payroll, gladly accepted the water without question. Thinking up a self-serving strategy to remove himself from prison time was hard work and had kicked up a thirst. Meeks watched Willie Boy consume the entire bottle before he made his way back to the sergeant's desk, where he spent his days fielding the precinct's calls and traffic.

After he was processed, Meeks overheard Willie telling one of the officers he needed to speak to Detective Payne. When asked why, Willie grinned. He had information in exchange for a deal. Meeks didn't bother calling the boss for instructions. It hadn't mattered what information Willie was willing to tell. Anything he said could be trouble for them both. The way he saw it, if he didn't take care of the problem now, they would all end up in jail; and there was no way he was going to let that happen.

∞

While everyone was back in lockup, witnessing Willie Boy's last breaths, a woman casually strolled through the squad room; stopping at Landon's jumbled desk. With a long, hot pink lacquered fingernail, she coolly picked through some of the files stacked there, while keeping an eye out for anyone returning to the area. Not finding what she wanted on his desk, she pulled open one of the draws and tried there. Retrieving one of the color coded files, she slipped it into her oversized shoulder bag. But before closing the drawer, she spotted the pen Landon's brother had given him and pocketed it too. Having found what she came for, she took her time heading for the exit. She only looked back once before pushing open the side door to the street. Thinking of her find *and* the pen, she smirked. She knew she shouldn't have taken it, but the designer pen was a nice one; much nicer than any she ever owned. Maybe one day she would buy Landon something equally nice as a trade. But today she had a job to do.

∞

After the death of his suspect and more frustrated than ever, Landon decided to stop by *Randy's Place* for some takeout before heading home. He was about to enter the restaurant when he did a double take at a man heading to his car. He hadn't seen his former colleague since the mess with Jess Ashford. Maneuvering his way between passing cars, Landon dashed across the street to catch up with an old friend.

"Rafe, Rafe Santiago," Landon called out just as Rafe was climbing into his car.

Rafe turned at Landon's shout.

"Hey buddy. I've been calling you for weeks now. What's going on?" Landon had tried calling; leaving messages; even visiting his home, but to no avail. He knew Rafe's firing had to be tough, but the Rafe he knew was tougher. And if it hadn't been for a miracle, he could have been in his friend's shoes.

"Hey Landon, man…"

Rafe stuck his hands in his pockets and slumped forward. He had no words. He could have returned his calls, but he didn't want to revisit his involvement with Jess and his subsequent firing from the department with Landon. Over the past weeks, he had run into some of the others from the department and the encounters had been uncomfortable to say the least. Some of his former colleagues were sympathetic, while others took his involvement as something to be joked about. To Rafe, his current unemployed status was no laughing matter. Not only had he lost his job, but he had also lost his family. As soon as his wife found out what he had done, she took their daughter and left town; leaving him to fight through this madness on his own.

Landon caught the gesture and fully understood. The man was embarrassed. "Look, you don't have to say anything. I understand. I just wanted to check up on you and see if there was anything that I could do. Have you found another job yet?" Landon was genuinely concerned. Jess Ashford had wrecked a lot of lives during her short tenure as the city's district attorney. Those lives would never be the same.

Rafe shook his head. "Nah, I'm still looking. Something will come up. I've even considered taking the fireman's exam and becoming a firefighter. Who knows? I just might make it." He chuckled uncomfortably. He had taken the exam and passed. He was just waiting to get a job offer. At the same time, he didn't want to work anywhere but MCPD.

What he really wanted was his old job back; but fooling around with Jess slammed that door shut for good.

It wasn't fair that he lost his position because of a fling with that whorish bitch. In his mind, Jess Ashford was the real villain in this whole ungodly situation. All roads to his downfall led back to her. He wouldn't even entertain the idea that all he had to do was refuse her offer to climb into her bed. But more importantly, there were others who were just as guilty. Others who managed to escape the consequences of cozying up to Jess's generous charms. This thought brought a fleeting display of anger that swiftly crawled across his face. It had come and disappeared so quickly, Landon thought he had imagined it.

Instantly regaining his composure, Rafe offered his friend an optimist grin. "Hey man, thanks for thinking of me. But you know me. I'll be back on my feet in no time."

Rafe clapped Landon on his shoulder before sliding into the driver's seat of his car. Landon nodded and watched him pull away from the curb. There was no doubt in his mind that Rafe Santiago would indeed recover from this mess. Although he still felt bad, he felt a little better after seeing him in the flesh. At least he was actively trying to correct his mistakes.

Frowning, Rafe watched while Landon crossed the street towards *Randy's* from his rearview mirror. He didn't need his pity. He didn't need him at all. He was going to make things right and get his family back. He was willing to do whatever it took to get his wife and child back in their home. His wife might be angry now, but once she saw that he was making amends, he would persuade her to come home. He made a mistake. He would convince her that he would never cheat on her again. But in the meantime, he had a plan forming to make *everything* right. Seeing Landon had renewed his drive as well as his confidence. Yes. Things were going to be just fine.

Chapter 3

Eric Valero sat in his office frustrated. They were no closer to solving the Kane case than they were months ago. And after yesterday's fiasco, he wondered if it would ever be solved. It was like someone was always a step or two ahead of them when it came to this case.

Tossing aside the report he was scrutinizing, Eric closed his eyes and sighed. The coroner had indeed cited foul play in his preliminary exam involving Willie Boy's death. From what she could tell, there may have been some sort of poison involved, but wouldn't know the source until the final tests returned. Just as he thought; poisoned, but how? The report claimed no puncture marks were found. Could he had absorbed it another way? Ingested it? And if so how? The man had only come in contact with a couple of officers after his initial arrest. Landon could vouch the man had nothing on him to suggest he poisoned himself, so how was it administered and by whom? The cell was thoroughly searched from top to bottom. And because that particular cell was in a newly renovated area of the building, surveillance cameras hadn't been installed yet. The company that was to place them had been dragging their feet for weeks. He asked the desk sergeant to make sure the job was done today. He didn't need any more foul ups.

Momentarily putting this new investigation on hold, Eric brought his thoughts to his upcoming nuptials. He was relieved he had his final tux fitting the day before. Although he was excited to be marrying the love of his life in a couple of days, he did not feel up to putting that suit on again until the ceremony. Anything short of that was unwelcomed at the moment. The death of Willie Boy had him on edge; anticipating the next blow in this perplexing case. But whatever was to come, he just hoped it would wait until after the wedding.

He checked his watch. He had a couple of hours before he and KT were to meet with the caterer to finalize the food for the reception. Eric relaxed. The thought of his fiancé brought a much welcomed smile. Kaitlin Ellis was about to become his wife. He grinned at the idea of having her under the same roof every day. He loved her too much to try to put into words the joy that one move would bring. He would spend the rest of his life proving that love in every way imaginable.

Still thinking of their wedding, he pulled open a desk drawer to retrieve the tickets for their trip. Although they planned the wedding together, he insisted he arrange their honeymoon on his own. He wanted it to be a surprise of a lifetime. They were destined to cruise the Mediterranean and then tour most of Europe. They would be gone for three glorious weeks and he couldn't wait to spend time alone with his soon to be wife.

Eric was brought out of his musings by a tap on his door. With a resigning sigh, he replaced the tickets before granting the visitor entrance. He didn't want anyone to catch wind of his surprise and spill the beans to KT. Just as he shut the drawer, the desk sergeant entered.

"I just wanted you to know, the last of the cameras are being installed as we speak. I had to replace the original contracted company with Graham Inc., who was more than punctual in performing the task. " Sergeant Meeks offered Eric a self-possessed smile. He was happy to give him the news. It no longer mattered that the area was now being monitored. His mission had been accomplished. Nodding at his superior, he was about to retreat back to his desk, when Eric asked him to stay and close the door behind him. Confidently, Meeks seated himself in one of the two chairs before Eric's desk.

"Owen, did you see anything suspicious happening yesterday, before Willie collapsed?" Eric considered Meeks a friend and saw no need to use titles when they weren't among their fellow coworkers.

Owen shook his head. "I've gone over it a thousand times, but there was nothing out of the ordinary. He was brought in, booked and placed in holding. He was back there for a while, before he asked to speak to Detective Payne. One of the officers assigned to that area delivered the message and returned to his post. After that…" Owen shrugged.

There wasn't any more he could tell him, literally. He just thanked his lucky stars he had the foresight to have ole Willie Boy placed in that blind spot or he wouldn't have been able to take care of him. Owen also failed to mention he relieved the two officers for break, before handing Willie the bottle of water.

Eric nodded. He knew if there was anything suspicious going on anywhere in the station, Owen was on top of it. He trusted him. He just couldn't figure out how anyone could have gotten to Willie.

∞

Sergeant Meeks returned to his post with a tight smile. He didn't feel one bit of remorse for lying to his "friend". The way he saw it, everyone had to look out for themselves. He liked Eric and thought he was a great boss. But the money he was paid for doing little to nothing, far out valued his so called friendship with his boss. Friends come and go, but opportunities like this only came once in a lifetime. Once he accrued enough money, he would quietly resign and live his dream of owning a ranch in Wyoming. Just a few more weeks and he should have enough to do just that and he couldn't wait. He was tired of Metro City and its problems. He wanted the quiet, peaceful life he dreamed of for years and it was just a few steps away. Owen Meeks' smirk turned into a full-fledged grin. He was about to retire and live the life he deserved.

Sergeant Owen Meeks had been with the Metro City Police Department for far too many years than he cared to remember. After quite a few of those years knocking heads and jailing undesirables (among other things), he had spent the remainder of his service behind the assignment desk, all due to a well-placed bullet.

Before landing at his current post, Meeks was considered one of Metro City's heroes and was well on his way to moving up the ranks within the department. There was even talk of him someday becoming commissioner with his exemplary record and commendations. But his dreams of a promising future were put to an end when he was shot.

Out on bail, one of the cons he put away had come gunning for him one night while making a stop before heading home. The man shot him in the chest; creating enough damage to put him on the sidelines instead of back on the streets with all the action—legal *and* illegal.

The shooter was heated for what Meeks stole from him during his arrest. Meeks and his then partner had stumbled upon a drug deal that netted copious amounts of drugs and untraceable quantities of cash. Unbeknownst to his partner, not only had Meeks confiscated some of the money for himself, but a fair amount of drugs which he tasked one of his street snitches to sell in Elgin, a city a hundred miles outside of Metro City.

When the suspect was taken to court and the charges were read, along with an itemized list of confiscated items, he knew Meeks or his partner had stolen from him. It hadn't mattered that he would never see the money or the drugs again. It mattered that dirty cops were getting away with what they arrested *him* for. He didn't even bother to mention it to his attorney or the officers' superiors. They would never take the word of a career criminal over their own. Upon his release, he decided to extract his own revenge. Unfortunately for him, he encountered Meeks first. The angry con followed Meeks to a neighborhood corner store. Before Meeks could step inside, the man called out and shot Meeks as he turned. Before he went down, Meeks was able to return fire killing the con instantly; allowing Meeks' secret to die with him.

After healing and finding himself permanently chained to a desk, Sergeant Owen Meeks thought his opportunity to fund his true dream had passed away also; that was before he was approached by Alec Campbell. Not only was the man paying him more money than he could ever score on the side in the streets, but he didn't have to lift a finger to collect it. All he had to do was be the mayoral hopeful's eyes and ears at police headquarters. And since he was in the perfect position to do just that, he jumped at the chance. He kept his head down and his eyes open and no one was the wiser. Unaware of his unscrupulous activities, everybody loved and trusted him. It was easy.

Sergeant Meeks grinned as he filed the completed paperwork for the newly installed video cameras. This job was too easy. He had managed to kill a man right under the nose of Metro City's top cops.

Chapter 4

"I would ask if you were excited, but from the sparkle in your eyes and that huge grin, I have my answer."

Blake Steele smiled at her newest friend. They were having lunch after KT's final fitting for her wedding gown. Blake hadn't known her long, but they took to each other immediately. They met soon after she and Kobe officially started dating. Blake was never one to have many friends and after she decided to move back to Metro City, Kobe thought she and KT would hit it off. In his opinion, the two women had a lot in common and he was right.

"Blake, I don't know if I could be any happier if I tried. I'm marrying a man that I didn't know even existed until a couple of years ago. I never thought I could love and be loved so thoroughly. Eric is more than I could have ever hoped for." KT closed her eyes; savoring the love and close bond they shared.

Remembering her friend, KT gave Blake a knowing grin. "But enough about me. I hear you and Kobe are getting along." She was happy for them, especially Kobe. They were all beginning to think he would never recover from Bria's death.

Blake blushed. Something she wouldn't have imagined herself capable of, before meeting Kobe. "Yes we are. And I am about to tell you something I just recently admitted to myself. I love him." Blake smiled at her admission. She liked the way it sounded. It was her first time saying it out loud and it felt perfect.

"Oh, I knew it! And the way he lights up when you are together, I think he loves you too. You two are so good for each other. I'm so happy for you both!" KT marveled at the change. Kobe was a very different man than when she first met him. Blake had managed to bring out the best in him and she thought it wonderful.

Blake smiled; reflecting on her own growth. "I must admit though; I wasn't the nicest person when Kobe and I first met. I'm pretty sure Eric has told you all about that." KT nodded. "But now, it's as if the old Blake never existed." She shrugged. It took a man like Kobe West to make her realize she deserved happiness too; despite what her mother believed. She leaned in for KT's reassuring hug. Her friend understood the individual struggles the couple had to endure to reach this point.

"Hey, hey…break it up you two."

KT regarded the newcomer with a chuckle. "Well speak of the devil." It was Kobe. He leaned down to kiss her on the cheek, before giving Blake a more personal greeting.

"Hey, what are you doing here?" Blake asked after a few seconds of his lingering kiss.

"I was headed to my car when I spotted you two through the window, so I decided to come and say hello." He kissed her once more.

Kobe never thought he could care for anyone again after losing Bria, but he had. And it was just as much a surprise to him as anyone else. Although he was drawn to

Blake when they first met, he couldn't have predicted they would be together. The old Blake Steele was about as obnoxious as they came. The woman was tall, shapely, beautiful and rich; and welded those formidable stats with unmitigated privilege. She and Kobe had clashed from the second they laid eyes on one another. He saw Blake as everything that Bria was not. Where Blake was brash and demanding, Bria was kind and giving. The contrast between the two was different to say the least. But after spending time with Blake and witnessing her interaction with her mother, Kobe saw her in a different light and quickly understood the source of her challenging attitude. That was the moment he knew he would have her in his life. As much as he wanted to be there to shield her from the older woman, he also sensed a way to change both of their lives for the better.

KT checked her watch. "Oh, here take my seat. I have to meet Eric for some last minute details." She rose from chair; grabbing her purse; hugging Blake simultaneously. "If I don't see you before, I will see you two at the wedding." She air kissed at Kobe and rushed out of the restaurant.

"Well isn't she the whirlwind?" Taking the proffered seat, Kobe shook his head. Since being engaged, KT had become all fluff and mush, something Kobe wouldn't have guessed if he hadn't witnessed it with his own eyes. KT's nature was to take it as it comes. But just like Blake, she too had softened.

As an afterthought, Kobe's brow bunched. "And was that a purse she was carrying?" he asked; indicating the expensive hand bag KT had casually slipped over her arm. Prior to Eric, she wouldn't have been caught dead with such an accessory. It clashed with her red and black, customized Ducati Super Sport motorcycle; a pre-wedding gift from Eric. Yes, this was definitely a softer, more feminine Kaitlin Ellis.

Blake laughed. "Oh stop and cut her some slack. The woman is in love, so she should be all gushy."

Kobe smiled at the melodic timbre of Blake's laugh. She was so different from the over-the-top woman he met months ago. Laughter looked good on her. His own eyes softened when he reached out to touch her face. She was beautiful. He ran a thumb across her cheek, before turning his attention back to her and KT.

"So what were you two talking about when I came in?" He was curious. They had their heads together as if sharing a secret.

Blake started to play it off but better of it. It was time she let him know how she felt. She opened her mouth to reveal her feelings for him when his phone chimed.

"Hold that thought." Kobe pulled the smart phone from his back pocket to answer it.

Blake could tell from his side of the conversation that he had to leave. It was just as well. When she told him she loved him, she wanted his undivided attention. Ending his call, Kobe shrugged his apology. And as she predicted, he was called back to the office. He kissed her again and promised to see her later that evening, before dashing for the exit. Having nothing else to do, she decided to stay and have coffee and dessert to ponder Kobe's reaction to her declaration. Just as the server placed her decadent order in front of her, she felt a presence behind her. Before she could turn towards the person, her mother stepped into view. Blake closed her eyes with inward dread. Not waiting to be invited to join her, Janice Steele made herself comfortable in the chair Kobe had vacated.

"Mother," Blake sourly greeted Janice with a frown hidden behind her raised coffee cup. She needed the strong espresso to steady her nerves. Janice Steele's presence was always an unhappy event.

Janice deftly dismissed Blake's less than warm reception. It was her lucky day in finding her only daughter at one of her favorite eateries. She had been trying to connect with Blake for days, but Blake had purposely ignored her calls. Janice should have taken it as a hint and left her alone, but she needed extra money for one of her many excursions.

"Blake dear, you haven't returned any of my calls. Did you get my messages?" Janice spoke to her daughter after detaining the server to order one of the restaurant's popular dishes with all the trimmings. She had settled in for the long haul; fully expecting Blake to pick up the tab.

Janice Steele never sought out her daughter unless it was to beg for money. Before her son Derrick's incarceration, her calls to her daughter were merely for the pleasure of inflating her own ego by deflating Blake's self-esteem. Blake erroneously assumed, once the monthly dispensed funds resumed, after Derrick's conviction, Janice would leave her alone as before. But she managed to manufacture reasons to contact her just the same.

Blake gave Janice her most disapproving scowl that was reserved only for her. "Yes mother, I did get your messages. The money you requested has been forwarded to your account just as you demanded." Blake glanced at her slice of cherry chocolate cheesecake. Suddenly it didn't seem so rewarding after all. Janice had managed to ruin that too.

Needing to change the subject, Blake took another sip of her coffee before she spoke again. "Have you bothered to visit your son since he's been in prison? He *is* the one footing the bill for your lavish lifestyle." Blake knew before she asked, she had not.

Blake was grateful that Derrick wanted to continue funding their mother's spending sprees. Even though she and her brother both had more money than either of them could spend in several lifetimes, she much preferred not having Janice's ungrateful hands in her pocket. If she'd had any say in the matter, her mother wouldn't receive one red penny. She didn't deserve it.

Janice sat ramrod straight, frowning with disdain. She placed the fresh napkin she demanded the server bring, onto her lap, before she answered. "You know I don't like visiting that place." She eyed her daughter while dramatically shuddering, before continuing.

"Why should I sully myself because he chose to be such a despicable person? There is no reason why I should visit him." She resentfully fidgeted in her chair at the very mention of such a gesture.

Blake stared at her mother with equal contempt. *No reason at all since you are still getting what you want out of him*, Blake thought. *You probably wish he would quietly and quickly die, so you can get your undeserving little hands on all of his money.*

Janice was intimate with the stipulations of Derrick's will. Should he pass away, under any circumstances, she would inherit his entire estate. And knowing Janice as she did, Blake wouldn't put it past her to wish her brother dead. The conniving bitch was just that callous.

Janice Steele was a taker and it didn't matter whose pockets she took from. Before Blake moved back to the states to handle her brother's affairs, Derrick was the one with whom Janice placed all of her demands; only contacting her occasionally. Her mother and brother had a strange relationship. Derrick didn't like Janice any more than she did. But for whatever reason, he put up with her, despite the fact he didn't need her.

Most of the people Derrick used were thrown aside once he was finished with them, but not Janice. She understood Derrick tolerating their mother growing up. It was part of his game plan in order for her to bail him out of whatever predicament he had gotten himself into. The tradeoff was mutual, since Janice had him in the perfect position to do whatever *she* wanted. But after he became one of the country's top attorneys, Blake didn't see why he needed to continue to cater to her whims, let alone the financial trust he had set up for her generous monthly stipends. Perhaps it was just out of habit?

Blake had cut all ties with her mother years ago. It had taken years of mental abuse and a marriage of convenience for her to finally see her way of escaping Janice's malicious grip. Blake spent nearly her entire lifetime being nitpicked and criticized by her mother for whatever imagined infraction that she could heap upon her. Things weren't so bad while her father was still alive. Even in his perpetual drunken state, he managed to keep Janice off of her.

But after Janice drove her husband to an early grave, via a liquor bottle, she turned her mental tirades fully onto Blake, leaving Derrick to provide for them, instead of taking a job to provide for her children. Though once Blake was able to procure her own job and fend for herself, it relieved little financial pressure from her brother. From the moment Derrick was forced into the role of provider of the house, Janice refused to fend for herself; depending solely on Blake and Derrick whether they liked it or not, as if they owed her something. And at the moment, her source of income was managed through Blake who hated every second of her charge. She thought about handing Janice the entire trust Derrick set up for her, just to get her out of her hair. But she quickly thought better of it; realizing Janice would still find a reason to harass her. Not to mention she probably would blow the whole wad just to get back at her.

Janice considered her daughter for a moment; studying her with an ever critical eye. Blake was young, beautiful, intelligent and wealthy; everything that she was not and she hated her for it. Janice viewed her daughter as competition from the moment Blake drew her first breath. Her husband Paul doted on their baby girl; giving her all of his attention while leaving Janice out in the cold.

Before Blake was conceived, Janice had Paul's undivided adoration. He gave her any and everything that she wanted; working endlessly to please her. But once Blake came into their lives, all of that changed. He abruptly cut back on his overtime hours, opting to spend more time with their daughter. Especially since Janice failed to give the girl any attention. She only attended to Blake if she was forced to. With Blake's arrival, Paul began to see his wife with new eyes. He saw the unrelenting selfishness that he couldn't control.

After Derrick was born, Janice found her revenge by taking him as her own pawn, in some diluted game to which only she knew the rules. She saw an opportunity to groom her son into giving her the attention she felt she deserved; driving her husband deeper into his drink of choice. And when Paul finally completed the task of drinking himself to death, Derrick was smoothly transitioned into his predetermined position with ease. But the regime change came with a hefty price. When Derrick found trouble, Janice was forced to become an ally in what she described as his boyish pranks. They had an unspoken agreement. As long as he continued to provide for her, she would continue to protect him in *anything* that he did. She even forgave him for that business with Tessa, knowing full well had she not he would have cut her off completely.

Now that Derrick was incarcerated for murder, among other things, her well-being was left to Blake, whom she knew despised the position, even though it was Derrick's money she was dispensing. This gave Janice all the more pleasure in needling her. But it seemed the bullying of her daughter was to be short lived. Somehow, during their years of separation, Blake had grown a backbone; she was not quite as malleable to her will as before. Blake stood up for herself; more so since she started seeing Kobe.

Janice didn't like the man and she knew the feeling was equally mutual, even though he never said or did anything that a casual observer would have noted to be off center. But Janice knew. It was the way he looked at her whenever she spoke to her daughter. There was great dislike and disapproval brewing just underneath the surface with that one. It was that disapproval that kept her from sauntering over to their table when she first entered the restaurant. She saw them immediately, but didn't dare approach Blake while Kobe was present.

Janice smiled at her daughter's discomfort and waved away her concern for not visiting Derrick. "But since you mentioned your brother, I want to talk to you about upping my allowance. I am sure Derrick won't mind if we change the terms a bit. Just mention it to him the next time you visit. Just think. If you give me more money, maybe I won't have to bother you so often."

Blake pushed away the now untouched dessert and nodded. She would agree to almost anything, if it meant less contact with Janice Steele.

Chapter 5

Syon followed Queen's line of sight until he spotted what had captured her attention. She was staring at one of the nurses who was leaving Metro Regional Hospital. He recognized the woman from a previous visit, after Queen was injured during a near miss by a likely distracted driver. The person who nearly ran her over was never found.

"Do you know her?" He asked

Queen slowly shook her head. "I don't think so, but she seems familiar somehow."

She and Syon were leaving the hospital as well. Syon had brought her there for Dr. Payne to give Queen the once over before their trip. Even though it had been weeks since the accident, Syon wanted to make sure nothing would come between them and the plans he'd made. They were heading to France for two weeks and he didn't want anything to spoil their time there. They both deserved a much needed get away. He'd visited the famous nation many times and wanted her to experience it through his eyes. He especially wanted them to enjoy hiking along the French countryside off the beaten tourist path. France had many scenic areas beyond Paris and the Eiffel Tower and he wanted them to take their time and cover as many as they could during their stay.

"You probably remember her from the last time you were here, which wasn't under the best of circumstances," he reminded. Although the danger had long passed, he was still concerned she was nearly killed in the street by some reckless driver. And it hadn't helped one bit that the driver was never apprehended. But since there hadn't been any other incidents, he had to be content that it was indeed an accident and she was safe. He made sure of it. There weren't many places she went that he wasn't right by her side. He almost lost her once, he wasn't about to leave it up to fate to take a second swipe at her.

"You're probably right." Queen took a last look at Shelby Kirkland before settling herself into the passenger's side of the Mercedes AMG SL, Syon's latest toy.

Syon too, gave the woman a last glance as Shelby lowered herself into her car. There *was* something familiar about her. It was as if he too had seen her before that day in the ER. Dismissing the strange sensation, he pressed the ignition button and pulled away from the curb. It was time to get their vacation started. He had a few more arrangements to make before leaving the next day; then they would be all set. He planned to propose to Queen while they were away and he had chosen a ring that was perfect for her. They may not have known each other long, but he was certain she was the woman for him. He didn't want to waste another moment thinking about a nurse or anyone else, when he had an engagement to prepare for.

∞

Shelby let herself into her new home. She was still getting used to it being hers, along with all the other things she inherited from her brother's death. Aside from the upscale condo, Kane left her all of his money and several vintage cars he had collected. She was in the process of

having most of them auctioned off. She had no need for
them. She offered to gift one of the expensive cars to Jon,
but he promptly declined. Even though he never said why,
she knew he didn't want people to think he was with her
because of her newly acquired wealth. He reminded her he
was more than able to purchase one of the vehicles he had
his eye on. In fact, he and his brother Landon both chose
cars and promptly gave her the asking price for each. She
had signed the final papers to turn the cars over to the
brothers earlier that day. But little did they know, in ninety
days her attorney would be returning both cashier's checks,
whether she and Jon continued to see each other or not. She
didn't need the money and it made her happy to gift the
cars to them.

Glad to be home, Shelby kicked out of her shoes
and padded across the lush carpet to press a shiny silver
button near the gourmet kitchen. The button quietly
released an intricately decorated, motorized panel. Once the
panel completed its trek along the hidden track, it revealed
a temperature controlled wine closet. She chose a bottle
from the extensive collection and poured herself a healthy
glass of an expensive Merlot, before settling on the pristine
white sofa. She lovingly brushed a hand across the lavish
fabric. Not only did her brother have excellent taste in
wine, but every piece of furniture and accent piece reflected
his surprising character. She wondered where he picked up
his taste for the finer things. Was it from their missing in
action mother or was it from their equally missing father.
Neither whom she knew.

Shelby sighed. Since Kane's death, her parents had been weighing heavily on her mind. She didn't know if either of them was still alive. She suspected her brother knew, and if she hadn't been so stubborn as to cut him out of her life, she could have made him tell her. But now that was impossible. She was aware that Jon had Landon looking into her parents' whereabouts, but his brother had hit a brick wall. And with everything else that had been going on, Landon hadn't had much time to spend on the task.

It was just as well. It was obvious they didn't want to be found so who was she to force herself into their lives. But still, she wondered if she had other siblings out there somewhere. Could her parents have met other people and had more children? Could her parents still be together? She may never know.

In the complete quiet of her musings, the chiming of the intercom startled her. She came to her feet to answer it. The doorman informed her Jon was on the way up. Shelby unlatched the door and stood it ajar before returning to her seat and her glass of wine. While she waited for Jon, Shelby remembered the feeling of someone watching her most of the day. Even though nothing or no one seemed out of the ordinary at the hospital, she still had that sensation of being observed. And it just wasn't today, but the feeling had been with her off and on for days. She made a mental note to be more aware of her surroundings. Although she couldn't think of any reason anyone would be following her, she would be vigilant just the same.

∞

Reclaiming her viewing spot, Jimi Leigh Tyler pulled up to the corner of the alley way facing the high rise building. Tossing a half-eaten glazed donut into a greasy bag, she pitched the entire thing into the back seat. She was getting pretty restless observing and not getting any *real* work in. Not to mention she hadn't had a decent meal in days. She hoped her next assignment would be more than collecting Intel and observation. She was itching for some action. What good was it to have such a skill set and not be able to use it? She was beginning to think she may have to rethink her current employment for something more hands-on.

Jimi's talents were many faceted. She was good at breaking and entering without leaving one iota of a trace behind. She was also a black belt in Ty kwon Do; her latest skill added to her repertoire of talents. It was more than apparent she could handle herself in any situation. But what rounded out Jimi's abilities was her extensive formal training.

Jimi Leigh Tyler was ex-military; trained in specialized combat, with the fluency of speaking several languages added to her impressive resume, which made sitting around in a car more sedate than she cared to be. But considering her last assignment, before leaving the Army, she needed the down time; her mental health demanded it. Even though she had been out of the game for nearly three years, Jimi still had nightmares from that last mission. The Intel her unit received had been disastrously erroneous, leading many in her squad wounded or killed. Having planned to retire from the Army, after a long and successful career, Jimi decided to review her options after the botched operation. So when the choice arose to continue her military career or leave for a calmer environment, Jimi chose the latter. She loved the Army, but enough was enough. She couldn't watch another friend die unnecessarily.

Although she considered her current assignment mundane, she thanked her lucky stars she had her life. If she had moved to the left three inches on that fateful day, she would not have been there to complain. But still, she felt she could be of more use if she was let off her leash.

But her client didn't want any hands on unless the situation became crucial. In her experience, by the time something became necessary it was usually too late. But she wasn't getting paid the big bucks to second guess her employer and the money *was* outstanding. After she finished this job she would be able to take her dream vacation to the islands of Hawaii. She had visited many countries during her stint in the Army, but had never had the opportunity to explore her own. Hawaii was just the first of many stops on her bucket list of places to visit. And after this job, she deserved it.

Jimi was about to check her watch for the nth time, wondering if her target was in for the night, when her mobile phone vibrated between her generous breasts. For her, there was no better place to keep it. Besides, it gave her a little thrill with each call. This was another reason

Jimi was glad to be free of military life. She could be more of herself. She may have missed the rush of the top secret missions, but she certainly didn't miss the required garb. Once she left her former life behind, she quickly adapted to a more comfortable code of dress. She chuckled the first time she donned a hot pink midriff top that displayed her tight abs and gold butterfly piercing. If her unit could see her now, they wouldn't be able to recognize her.

Popping the grape flavored gum she was chewing, Jimi let the phone vibrate a few seconds more before retrieving it with her long, curved hot pink nails. She checked the caller display; just like clockwork it was her client. And as usual, her report would be the same. *Nothing to report.*

Jimi ended the call just as Jon Payne turned into the visitor's parking garage. The fact that he parked in the garage and not in the circular drive, meant the couple were probably in for the evening. Usually when he and Shelby were doing a night on the town, she would be waiting for him out front; but not tonight. She would give it another hour and then she would go home to get a real meal and catch a couple of hours of sleep before moving on to the next task. But while she waited, there was one more chore she needed to complete.

Jimi exited her non-descript, late model, American made car and took her time crossing the street, with her jean-clad rounded bottom swaying with every step. She was careful to avoid the surveillance cameras around the place. It wouldn't do her any good to be captured on one of those things. She needed to stay invisible. Once inside, she spotted the good doctor's car. Careful to avoid the inside cameras as well, Jimi crouched low as she maneuvered her way to the doctor's parking spot. Pulling back her long micro braided tresses, she stooped down to place a device on the car's undercarriage. With the mission accomplished, she sashayed her way back to her car. After another forty-five minutes and no Shelby, she started the car and pulled from the curb. Her work here was done for the night.

Chapter 6

Alec was restless. Officer Owen Meeks had moved a little too swiftly for his taste. He appreciated the man's take charge initiative, but he still needed to be kept in the loop. He was paying Meeks after all.

Although irritated, Alec had to agree; Willie had become a loose end, but did the man have to kill him inside the police station? With Willie dead and his number one man unaccounted for, there were too many unfulfilled tasks for his comfort. He wondered if Meeks was up to his standards or did he have to call in a favor from another heavy hitter. He dismissed the notion of needing to bring in yet another person to this already chaotic mess. He had to believe Meeks was safe. No one within the police department was aware of his connection and he could count on the man to make sure it stayed that way.

He sighed. This was becoming more than he bargained for. Maybe he should have just handled everything himself then there wouldn't have been any loose ends or rogue allies to worry over. At any rate, both jobs needed to be done and done competently, as well as quickly; no more mistakes. At this late moment in the game, he couldn't afford another mishap.

Even though he was anxious, Alec had to count his blessings in spite of the delay. His previous hire had been able to obtain Queen Willis's birth certificate, and yes, as he suspected, Maureen was Queen's mother, but the space for birth father had been left empty. Nonetheless, even without written confirmation, he knew Queen was his daughter. Her age and the time frame in which he and Maureen were together, fit. The affirmation was proven 100% after the DNA test came back. His former associate did have the good sense to swipe some of her blood from the hospital after the accident, before he vanished for good.

He still had no idea where the man ran off to. After that last stunt he pulled, without his sanction, he disappeared without a trace. If he had known the man would become a loose cannon, he would never have shared a certain tidbit of information with him. He couldn't blame him for wanting revenge, but on his own dime and not his. Just when he thought he could take a relieved breath that things were running smoothly, his associate became a new problem. For his sake, Alec hoped he was rotting in a ditch somewhere.

Putting the whereabouts of his last contractor on the back burner, for now, Alec returned to his current problem. Since he hadn't known of his daughter with Maureen, it was safe to say maybe Queen didn't know he existed either. She didn't appear to recognize him that one time he encountered her; even with him staring at her. But he couldn't take that chance. He did not need any children of any kind to be linked to him. That was a thread he couldn't afford to be pulled. And although his opponent in the mayor's race was playing nice at the moment, things could easily turn ugly since he was losing in the pre-election polls. Hamilton may want to start digging for dirt; at least that's what he would do if the circumstances were reversed. Even though Ryan Hamilton wasn't the favorite in the race, he wasn't backing down. It appeared he wanted the job as mayor just as much as he did. Alec figured the man must have his own ambitions. And just like his former associate, Ryan Hamilton was unpredictable. He didn't need him or anyone else looking into his background too deeply, even though he was certain he had covered all his tracks, it didn't hurt to be too careful.

After calming his doubts over Meeks with a shot of whiskey, Alec picked up the phone one last time in hopes of reaching his rogue operative. If he didn't make contact this time, he better hope like hell he was dead, because if he wasn't, at some point in the near future he would be.

Chapter 7

Rafe Santiago looked at his phone for what seemed like the hundredth time—Alec again. He had no intentions of answering him, ever! After settling the score with Eric Valero and Landon Payne, he would be paying his former employer a last visit, but not now. He had other work to do. He knew Alec was about to explode because he dropped out of sight, but he would get over it. He was done with him once he learned he was the cause of him losing his job. The money Alec had already paid him was good, but would only sustain him for so long. Besides, the way he saw things now, it wouldn't have matter what he paid him. He liked his job as a police officer and Alec had taken that away from him. No, money was good, but revenge was better.

Rafe started working for Alec after "that bitch," as Jess Ashford had come to be known, dumped him. Although he knew the hookup with the former sexy DA was short term, it didn't sit too well that she immediately moved on to his good friend Landon Payne. Whereas he and Jess only slept together a couple of times, she allowed Landon in her bed night after night, even when he was supposed to be on patrol.

What did Landon have that he didn't? He couldn't understand why she chose Payne. Why did he have a privilege that was denied him? He was better looking than Landon and he was more accessible, considering he was her bodyguard and driver. No one would have questioned why the city owned vehicle was parked in her driveway at any given time. It was his job to make sure she was safe and secure when he brought her home. He was expected to enter her house and stay if necessary given the death threats she received over her tough crime crack down and prosecutions. Landon, on the other hand, could have been caught multiple times over if the wrong person happened to venture upon Jess's house in the middle of the night and found him in a division he was not assigned.

So when Alec approached him for the job of spying on the whore of Metro City, he gladly accepted. Especially after learning Alec would use the information to bring Jess down. But unknown to him at the time, his transgressions with the woman had also been documented. Alec had tasked Meeks to place hidden cameras in Jess's house, before she moved in. Rafe didn't find out about *his* video with the lady prosecutor, until after the entire collection was leaked for the whole world to see; well, almost the entire collection.

He had been off duty the day the unfortunate mess hit the fan. He was trying to grab a few more hours of sleep when his wife attacked him. His wife, Elaina, had just put their daughter on the bus to school, when her cell phone exploded with a series of calls and texts. Curious, she clicked on the last text sent. Attached was the damning time and date stamped video of him and Jess having sex in her bedroom. She only had to click on the one to get the gist of the others. After viewing the eye opening clip, Elaina didn't take the time to ask any questions. She marched right into their bedroom and clocked him in the head with the offending phone. She cursed him in English and Spanish as she pounced on the bed; laying into him with both fists. It took him several minutes to calm her down enough to understand why she was upset.

He would never forget that day. Following one of the links on Elaina's phone, it had only taken him a few seconds to recognize himself in the video posted on that trash site *Do Tail*. All the blood had drained from his face the instant his eyes landed on his moment of shame. His sins had been displayed in living color for the entire world to see *and* hear via the supplied raunchy audio. The website didn't even bother to blur out the various connected and unconnected body parts. It was displayed "as is". The only warning the viewer received that he or she were about to witness real life porn, was a small ticker that streamed a disclaimer at the beginning of the montage of their faces and asses.

While Rafe watched in horror, Elaina had retreated into the bathroom, crying uncontrollably. When the land line began to chime, then *his* cell, he knew there was no escaping the damning evidence. He didn't have to be a psychic to know what the calls were about. Knowing he had to try to get ahead of it the best way he could, he called the precinct only to learn he had been placed on administrative leave until further notice. And that further notice came the next day via express mail; documenting his subsequent firing for behavior unbecoming of a police officer and dereliction of duty, since technically he was on the clock when he was screwing the lady DA. And if that wasn't bad enough, Elaina packed up his daughter and moved to her mother's, several states away.

After he lost his job and his family had left, he started working for Alec full time; throwing himself into his work to take his mind off of his dilemma. It was later, much later when he found out the ugly truths. Before Jess's ugly unveiling, he was under the impression she had just slept with him, that lawyer and Landon, never even giving much thought as to anyone outside of Metro City. But the truth was more horrible than he could have imagined. Alec Campbell knew Jess Ashford had slept with half the world and had the evidence to prove it. Not only had he been just another pawn in Jess's head games (literally and figuratively), but also in Alec's agenda. Alec wanted Jess gone from Metro City. He needed her gone if he was to become its next mayor and he used him to accomplish this task. It wasn't enough that he had proof of her sleeping with various men in other cities, hell in other countries; he needed documentation that she was peddling her wares in Metro City as its district attorney as well.

Rafe was livid. Alec had much more on Jess than he could have ever dreamed; leaving him unprepared for the worst case scenario if any of Alec's evidence was ever discovered. It was when he learned *how* it was discovered that he went off the rails. Alec had sent the entire lot to Eric Valero, including the video he had of him! He should have killed Alec right then and there, but at the time his rage had been focused on Valero; Detective Eric Valero and how he protected Landon and not him. And when Landon made detective he finally knew why. Eric had been grooming Landon for a spot on his team, so there was no way he would let his heir apparent fall.

Rafe knew it was past time that he got even with his former boss and buddy. Nothing else mattered for him. But when it was all said and done, Alec Campbell would be his last stop on his trek of revenge. He would make sure the man suffered greatly.

Gathering his thoughts as well as plans, Rafe begin his mission. It was time to shift into overdrive and stay there until every detail of his carefully mapped out plan was executed.

Yes, it was time to make them all pay!

Chapter 8

Slowly opening his eyes, Syon blinked. He had lost consciousness and now couldn't get his mind to comprehend what was wrong and something was definitely wrong. It took him a full minute to realize he was hanging upside down; held in place by his seat belt. All at once the reason slammed into his consciousness with a hard and steady pounding. The car had crashed. With this thought came another. *Where was Queen!*

They were on their way to the airport when they were hit by something. Another car? He didn't know. There they were; driving along and he had turned to say something to her, when there was a huge ear splitting explosion, after which everything went dark. He didn't know how long he had been out, but any length of time was too much for him.

Syon steadied his head. The pounding was so great he couldn't keep his eyes open, but he had to. He had to see about Queen. Swallowing, he opened his eyes again; turning his head with the greatest of care, he blinked again to gain focus. Each small movement caused greater pain. When he was finally able to look to left, he saw her. She too was held by her seat belt, but there was a huge gash across her forehead at the base of her hairline. The cut was so precise it looked as if someone started to scalp her. He made himself turn to look at the windshield where most of the glass was scattered throughout the car. He deducted she had been cut by flying glass. Blood was streaming from the wound, along the strands of her hair and pooling on the car's ceiling.

Syon tried reaching for her, but cried out in pain instead. The movement brought him to realize his arm was likely broken. He tried calling out to her, but she didn't move or answer. Despite of his own pain, he continued calling to her, until several people came to their aid, with one of them asking if he was alright. He wasn't concerned for himself; he wanted them to help Queen. The good Samaritans pried the driver's side door open; carefully releasing him from his seatbelt and pulling him from the wreckage, with him wincing from his injuries. Syon tried to get to his feet, but the pounding and dizziness in his head wouldn't allow it. He soon accepted he had to depend on the strangers to help Queen.

Unlike Syon, Queen's predicament wasn't quite so easy to solve. After trying to get to her from the passenger side without any luck, the group had to wait for the first responders to arrive. Her side of the car was pushed in and held shut by the front end of another car. Once the fire department arrived, they worked to exact Queen while the paramedics attended to Syon's injuries. He had been punched in the face pretty good by the airbag, and the car flipping over, didn't help the situation. His arm wasn't broken. It had only been knocked free from the shoulder's socket. The paramedics placed his arm in a sling until they could get him to the hospital. Syon fought aid and unconsciousness to keep from being taken from the scene, but he was out voted by both. Realizing he was losing the battle, he asked one of the police officers, who had retrieved his phone, to call his brother Matthias. He wanted someone he could trust to be with Queen until he was able himself. Syon watched the woman while she spoke to his brother as he was lifted into the ambulance. He breathed a small sigh of relief. Queen wouldn't be alone. This was his last thought before the excruciating pain dragged him under a second time into blackness. Syon had lost consciousness.

∞

Matthias was on the scene shortly after Syon left in the ambulance. He couldn't believe anyone survived after observing the crushed car first hand. Even more so after the effort it took the firefighters to safely remove Queen from the destroyed vehicle. Once she was removed, the paramedics quickly went to work. At first he didn't think she was alive. She was so still and lifeless. But once one of the men confirmed he felt a pulse, he released the breath he hadn't realized he was holding; silently thanking God for the miracle.

Before climbing into his own car, to follow the ambulance to the hospital, Matthias's eyes wandered back to the totaled vehicle. The scene didn't make any sense. They were hit with such force that the car had flipped over unto its roof. If the car crash was caused by the other mangled car on the scene, why was it pressed against the passenger side door? With the car landing on its top, wouldn't that mean Syon's side of the car should have been perpendicular to the front end of the other car? It was as if someone drove around to Queen's side to do what...*finish the job?*

Matthias didn't like where his thoughts were heading. On a hunch, he took photos of the scene while the firefighters were working to get Queen free. He was told by more than one person that the front of other car had been rammed against her side of the vehicle. It was the reason Samaritans had to wait for the fire department to arrive. When he talked to the police on the scene, he learned the driver of the other car, a heavy duty utility truck, was long gone. He shook his head and started his car. He would worry about the contradictions later. He just hoped the doctors were able to keep Queen alive.

∞

"How is she? Where is she?" Syon had removed his IV and descended on his family the moment the doctors turned their backs. They were probably looking for him, as he had not been released from care. Syon tumbled into a nearby chair in the quiet waiting room. He was still feeling the effects of his head trauma.

"Hey buddy, what are you doing walking around?" Matthias helped him settle into the cushioned chair.

"Syon, are you alright? We were so worried." This was from his sister Paige. She and her husband Anderson Stone rushed to the hospital the moment Matthias called.

Fighting a wave of nausea, Syon held up his hand, as if to stop their words from piercing his throbbing skull. "I'm okay. What about Queen? How is she?" His eyes narrowed as he caught the exchange between his siblings. He knew that look. Something was wrong. "Tell me!" He repeated the command, but this time not much more than a whisper, to keep the pain from stabbing his brain again.

Matthias sat down next to his brother. The news was grim. "Sy, Queen's in a coma. She took the brunt of the crash. The vehicle that hit you struck on her side. Her right arm and leg are broken in several places. Her head was cut by flying glass and her brain sustained serious injury from being bounced around in her skull. She has a lot of healing to do." He didn't dare share his theory of someone was trying to kill her. He didn't even mention it to his sister or brother in-law. He needed time to investigate.

"What else?" Syon knew his brother well enough to know he was holding something back. And the look on Paige's face, along with her wet eyes confirmed it. She had been crying.

Matthias looked at his shoes before answering. Raising his head to meet his brother's gaze he told him. "Queen was pregnant Sy. I'm sorry, but the trauma...she lost the baby." He clasped his brother's shoulder, while Paige slid into the chair on his other side and hugged him; both gestures displaying their love for their brother.

Syon froze; dividing his questioning gaze between his brother and sister, who continued to hold on to him. Due to the pain still coursing through his head and just plain disbelief, he was having a difficult time comprehending Matthias's words. He replayed what he said syllable by syllable, until he understood the cruel truth.

Returning with coffee, Anderson observed the solemn scene and knew Syon had been told about the loss of his child. He quietly set the cups down on a nearby table and sat next to his wife, who had begun crying again.

Syon, struggling with his emotions, tried to rise. He didn't care how dizzy he was, he needed to see Queen; be with her. "Where is she?" Matthias tried pushing him back into the chair.

"I just talked to one of the nurses. Queen's still in surgery. They are trying to repair the damage." This was Anderson. "She also told me they've discovered some internal bleeding which is complicating things. I'm sorry Sy."

With the full force of the day landing on him, Syon dropped back into his chair and wept.

Chapter 9

Rafe Santiago stared down the scope and ground his teeth as he watched his former boss and friend walk towards their car parked in front of the building across the street. His jaw throbbed as he clenched tighter. Taking his finger from the trigger, he reflected on how easy it would be to pick them both off, right here and right now. But he wouldn't; not now any way. For one thing, when he took them out he wanted to make a clean getaway. If he killed them in front of the police station he was sure to be caught. Every cop in the building would be swarming the area within seconds. And unlike the shots he had taken during the ambush, his former brothers and sisters in blue were more alert now. At the apartment building, they never suspected or saw it coming. And if it hadn't been for Valero's quick thinking in pulling Landon to safety, Landon would be dead now.

It wasn't fair that Landon got to walk away from the circus his former boss created. And if it hadn't been for Valero, he wouldn't have. He knew the man had favorites and he knew Landon was one of them. He just hadn't realized to what lengths the detective was willing to go to protect his precious Landon Payne. He could have done the same for him but he chose not to. And for that he would pay.

As for Landon, the world seemed to have been laid at his feet. His good looks and easy going demeanor got him places and positions Rafe didn't think he deserved. He was just as good a cop as Landon and should have been considered for promotion as well. And even though he liked his job as body guard for the former DA, he could have used the bump in pay to help his family. He had dreams and aspirations just like Landon. Rafe thought if he had been considered for detective and promoted, he probably would never have slept with that skank Jess. He would have had better things to do, like making a better life for his wife and child. They would have been able to take more trips and buy nicer things. Hell, if he had even been considered for the position, he would have never taken up with Alec Campbell.

Rafe considered his wife and daughter. Alana vowed to never to return, because of his indiscretion. She may have been able to get past his cheating given time, if the world hadn't been privy to the whole mess. She wanted to distance herself and their child from him as much as possible. Everyone in her family hated him and would gladly beat the hell out of him if given half a chance. It was safe to say, he had lost his family for good.

He grunted with renewed anger. Yes, he could have been just like Payne, but Valero couldn't be bothered with what he needed or wanted. It hadn't mattered that he had a family that should have been protected from Jess's circus. For Eric, everything was about his 'favorite son' and that precious fiancé of his. Thinking of KT, Rafe suddenly had a better idea of dealing with Eric. Yes, he had something much worse than death in mind for him. He nodded with each new detail that formed in his new plan. This new idea of handling Eric Valero was much better. This way he could make a better impact. As for Landon, his plans for him would not change. He wanted to hurt them both without anyone suspecting Kane's killer was involved. As far as they were concerned Kane's killer was a ghost and he wanted to keep it that way. He would get his revenge when they least expected it.

Peering through the scope a final time, he mouthed the explosion of a single bullet that could pierce Landon Payne's heart, ending him forever.

Chapter 10

Kobe and Matthias sat in Eric's office. They were there to get information about the accident. The more Eric explained, the more they were perplexed. From all accounts this was no accident. Just as Matthias suspected, this may have been deliberate.

Eric explained that the driver of the other car vanished moments after the impact. And because that stretch of highway was mostly deserted at that time of morning, none of the people who stopped to help saw the driver. And to make matters worse the truck had been stolen days ago.

"The forensics team went over the entire vehicle but no prints were found, not even the owner's, who couldn't have escaped the scene if he had been driving. The man who owns the work truck is incapacitated due to a fall he'd taken on a job the previous week. He has a broken hip and is simply unable to drive. It looks like the truck had been stolen from his place of business. And if it hadn't been for the crash, he might not have known it was missing for weeks. The owner is a local self-employed plumber without any other employees. Therefore he wouldn't have missed it until he was back on his feet to work."

Eric rocked in his chair while the two men digested the news. All of this was too coincidental and he didn't believe in coincidences. With Queen being the common denominator, he had to rethink her last incident with the supposed texting driver. He now believed that was no accident either. He was beginning to believe someone wanted her dead and this time they nearly succeeded.

And as if reading his mind Matthias spoke up. "Here, you should see these." He handed Eric the printed photos he shot of the scene.

Eric took his time to scrutinize each one. He immediately saw the anomaly as Matthias had. There was no way this was an accident. By driving around to the passenger side, *after* the initial contact, the perpetrator was clearly trying to end Queen's life. Syon was just collateral damage. But why?

"Do you see it?" Matthias asked.

Eric slowly nodded. "Let me hang on to these. The officers who worked the accident weren't equipped to photograph the scene so these will come in handy in the investigation." Eric made a mental note to reprimand the two young officers later.

"Sure, whatever it takes to get to the bottom of this. I've carefully questioned Syon, but he couldn't think of any reason someone would do this on purpose. Although he is too worried about Queen to really give it much thought right now, I really don't think he has a clue either. This is all about Queen. For some reason someone wants her dead."

Matthias was relieved his brother was preoccupied for the moment. He didn't dare mention the contradictions in the accident scene or his suspicion that Queen was in more danger than any of them thought. He didn't need for him to go off and mess up the investigation. If they are to get answers, Syon needed to stay completely out of it.

"How is Syon handling all of this?" Eric finally asked.

"He's feeling helpless. He's taking it hard that they lost their child." Matthias felt powerless to the fact he couldn't help his brother.

"Any change in her condition?"

Matthias shook his head. "She's still in a coma. They may have to do more surgery if her brain starts to swell. The doctors are watching that closely. She is by no means out of the woods. Her situation will be critical for some time."

Kobe was deep in thought while the two men talked. *Why would someone want to kill Queen? That is the key to this.* He would look into Queen's background to see what he could come up with. He knew the police would be looking into it too, but there may be avenues he could cover that they couldn't.

After getting what information they could about the accident, Matthias and Kobe left. Once they reached the parking lot Matthias spoke.

"I want you to—"

"I'm already on it." Kobe already knew where to start. He had to make sure Allison St. James was still locked away.

∞

Eric continued to rock in his chair long after Matthias and Kobe left. He too wanted to know why eliminating Queen was so important and who stood to gain from her death. He already had someone looking into her original incident when she was nearly run down while crossing the street. He could kick himself for not looking into the incident further. But like everyone else, he thought it was what it appeared to be; some distracted driver not paying attention. The initial incident was months ago. And it didn't help that nothing else occurred until now.

He felt bad for Syon. After the accident, they found proof in Queen's luggage that she had planned to share her pregnancy on the trip. She had packed a bag of hints complete with cards and gag gifts to surprise him. Now there was no baby, not to mention Queen was fighting for her life. Whoever this bastard was, he hoped they found him soon. Each moment he or she remained at large, the more chances they had to try again. If it was important for them to attempt a second time, what would stop them from trying a third?

But now that they knew for certain someone was out to hurt her, Matthias had hired around the clock guards to insure her safety, not to mention a host of friends and family to keep an eye on her. As far as Syon knew, the protection was for the both of them until the culprit was caught. Matthias wanted his brother in the dark as much as possible to keep him from interfering. Eric and Matthias both vowed the person or persons would not get another attempt on Queen's life. Not on their watch. On Eric's part, he had dropped the ball once, but never again.

Eric glanced over at a tap on his door. "Come in." The strain of this case left him once his visitor stepped through the door. With a wide grin, he rose to greet his fiancé. Pulling KT into his arms he kissed her before either of them spoke.

"Now that's more like it. I needed that." Eric rubbed her back as he pulled away. But not ready to lose the connection just yet, he held her close again.

KT's smile turned grim. "I just left the hospital. Queen isn't doing so well." She was thinking how great it was that Queen had so many people who cared for her. She was equally grateful she had Eric

Eric nodded. "I know. Matthias and Kobe just left. They told me." Eric swiped at the helplessness that had returned to his chiseled features. "Is Syon still there? He needs to get some rest."

"Yes he is, along with Myka and Cymone. He's technically still a patient, so to not have to fight him any longer, Jon Payne arranged for them to be in the same room. The move seemed to work, because the moment he climbed onto his bed next to Queen, he fell asleep. The man was exhausted. I can't imagine what he's going through. It's one thing to have your future fiancé in a coma but to have lost a child?" KT shook her head.

"Don't tell me. He was going to propose on this trip?"

KT nodded. "Yeah, this was supposed to be a trip of a lifetime for them both. Listen, the reason I came by, I wanted to talk to you about our wedding tomorrow. I know that it's a bad time to leave, so I propose we have the ceremony as planned, but postpone the honeymoon until later. After this latest drama, a lot of us need to break some of this tension and a big party could be just the thing. What do you say?"

Eric slowly nodded. He could go for that. They did have everything in place, with people coming in from everywhere for the ceremony. It would be a stress reliever. This city could use some joy in the midst of the madness right now.

"Okay, you've got it."

"There's just one thing. Myka doesn't want to leave Queen not even for a few minutes and I understand, so I will be standing alone without a best woman and I am fine with it," she informed him.

He pulled her in for another kiss. "As long as you are there nothing else matters."

Chapter 11

The Wedding

"I think it was a great idea that you decided to go ahead with the wedding. Now that your honeymoon has been postponed, have you revealed to KT where you're taking her when this mess is over?" Justin Graham was helping Eric into his evening jacket.

Eric grinned. "Nope. It's still a secret and I plan on keeping it that way." He tugged on his sleeves as he glanced in the mirror. He too was grateful for moving ahead with the wedding. The joy of soon having KT as his wife was the most relaxed he'd been in weeks. Most grooms were nervous, but he was at peace.

"Does it look as if most of our guests have shown up?" It really didn't matter to him if no one came, as long as his bride would be walking down that aisle to greet him.

"How about I go check and give you a minute to yourself?" Justin clasped him on the shoulder before leaving the room.

∞

"Oh my goodness, you look so beautiful!" Blake was admiring KT's reflection in the full length mirror.

KT too was taken with her mirror image. This had to be the frilliest thing she had ever worn in her entire life and she loved it. But what she loved more was Eric Valero. In a few moments she would be Mrs. Valero. KT grinned at the new title.

Still gazing at herself, she addressed Blake. "Have you told Kobe how you feel yet?" She hoped to be attending their wedding soon.

Blake shook her head. "Not yet, but I will."

KT turned at this revelation, perplexed. "What are you waiting on?" She knew she loved him, so why was she holding back?

"Well you know that day we had lunch after your fitting?" KT nodded. "Kobe had to leave, but we made plans to see each other later that day and I had planned to tell him then. I was sitting there about to enjoy the dessert I'd ordered when who but my mother invited herself to my table. It was downhill from there."

KT groaned. Not only had Blake explained her relationship with Janice Steele, she had the displeasure of seeing the woman in action after Blake's brother was arrested. It was not a pretty sight.

"Well, you make sure you tell him soon. And please don't let your mother get you down. I understand how she is, but you shouldn't let her or anyone else get in the way of your happiness." KT felt for her friend. Janice Steele was indeed a piece of work.

Blake knew she was right. Janice had taken quite enough of her joy over the years and it was time that she stopped her in her tracks completely. It was easier dealing with her when they didn't live in the same country. But now that she was back living in Metro City, Blake needed a permanent solution for Janice's selfish demands in order to move on with her life. And she hoped that move would include Kobe.

She smiled at the thought of the man she loved. KT was right. She had wasted enough time. She would tell him today after the ceremony. She loved him and it was time that he knew it.

Chapter 12

Virginia Cooke sat quietly while the musical prelude played softly in the background. Although she knew a few people there, she wasn't really in the mood to strike up a conversation while she waited for the ceremony to begin. In fact, she didn't even know why she was there. She had no desire to attend someone else's wedding. She would be twenty-nine in a couple of weeks and still single. She thought Justin would have proposed by now, but he hadn't. They had been together nearly three years with no signs of him moving towards that coveted goal. And to make matters worse, she felt he wasn't going to. She could feel him losing interest with each passing day.

Before she left to take care of her ailing mother, she thought it was her imagination that he had become distant. But while she was away, they barely had a decent conversation. Sure she was busy helping her mother convalesce, but she still found time to pick up the phone to connect, with most of her calls going straight to voicemail. And when they did connect, he was always in a rush to end the conversation. When she returned, the strain between them grew even more. She was hoping the distance would have brought them closer. But when he came home to find her seductively draped across his bed, wearing little more than a smile, he feigned exhaustion; leaving her alone with the television while he showered and fell into bed to sleep.

Virginia sighed. She could think of a million things she could be doing instead of sitting there pretending to be happy for the perfect couple. KT was beautiful and her fiancé Eric, Justin's best friend, was every conscious woman's dream. The two were the most loving, stylish, compatible couple she knew. She was happy for them, but she would have been happier if it were *her* preparing to walk down that aisle in a beautiful gown.

When she first moved to Metro City, she had to admit she didn't know the first thing about fashion. Her former employer, Justin's former wife, made it impossible with the drab uniforms she made her wear. But all that changed once she started working for Justin.

At the time, her idea of couture was a pair of casual slacks with a halfway decent top to get by. She hadn't bothered to change her so-called style. And since she never ventured far from the house, she never needed to upgrade her wardrobe. But once she and Justin became involved, she had to do better. He was a mover and a shaker in the community, with him always attending lavish events and wanting her by his side. So after a couple of shopping trips and a few pointers from KT, she soon caught on and Justin had loved the transformation. He enjoyed showing off his beautiful girlfriend. But now, she could walk around naked and he wouldn't even give her a casual glance.

Absently smoothing down the lap of her perfectly tailored dress, Virginia glanced around the beautifully decorated garden. She noticed no expense had been spared and wondered just how much money had Eric spent to pull this off. The wedding was being held at the old Powers' estate, an odd choice considering what all had happened there. Virginia thought it should have been the last place for KT and Eric to consider a wedding, especially considering their involvement in the whole mess. But after a moment, she quickly reconsidered. Maybe it was *because* of their involvement that they chose the extravagant mansion.

She mentally shrugged. It could very well be their way of dispelling bad Karma or something. But still. Even though it had changed hands a few times, it was still referred to as the place where multi-millionaire Devin Powers held his fiancé and her lover hostage. And if today's crowd was any indication that the estate's atmosphere could be changed, the current owners were making a killing renting it out for occasions such as this. It was a shock to discover the place was booked solid for the next three years. Instead of turning people off, because of its history, most of Metro City would kill at the chance to take a peek inside the infamous mansion. So there were more than enough attendees for the big day. Eric must have had to pull some mighty big strings to have the wedding added to an already booked venue.

Virginia sighed before glancing over her should and was stopped short by a man who caught and held her gaze. She unconsciously repositioned herself to get a better look at her captive admirer.

Hmm...nice.

The man's enticing lips slyly lifted into an infectious grin which she found herself returning. Virginia absently smoothed down one side of her elegantly cut bob. She recognized him from various newspapers and television clips, but never had the pleasure to gaze upon the man in the flesh—until now. Ryan Hamilton was gorgeous. His hazel eyes continued to hold hers, as his smile widened.

This might not be a wasted afternoon after all, Virginia mused.

She was still eyeing Ryan when she heard her name being called. Virginia stuck a placeholder into her growing curiosity over the interesting Ryan Hamilton, to reluctantly turn to see who was trying to get her attention. When she met the attention seeker's gaze, she frowned. It was Justin.

Now he wants my attention? With those hazel eyes and intoxicating smile temporarily forgotten, Virginia turned fully towards Justin.

"You look uncomfortable, maybe I shouldn't have dragged you along," Justin was saying. He briefly glanced around the garden; noticing all the other attendees were engaged in various pockets of conversation. While Eric was having a moment to himself, he had come out to check on her, only to find her sitting alone.

"No, no. I'm fine…I'll be fine. You don't have to be worried about me. Just go on and fulfill your best man duties." A little flustered by his untimely attention, Virginia absently straightened his tie at the memory of why they were there. Her frown deepened. The gesture was a stark reminder that *she* wasn't the one getting married.

Resisting a frown of his own, Justin caught the reaction that played across her features and didn't have to guess its source. They would have to talk later. After rebuffing her latest attempts to rekindle the fire they once had, he'd made up his mind. It was time to end this. It wasn't fair to string her along any further. Virginia clearly wanted what he was not willing to give. It was only fair that he gave her the opportunity to find someone who was willing to be her everything.

"We'll talk later." Pulling away from her ministrations, he kissed her forehead before making his way up the aisle to greet a group of arriving guests. He stopped momentarily to shake hands with Ryan before continuing on.

Everything else forgotten, Virginia's frown remained on the chaise kiss, which was more like the kiss of death. It more than signaled their relationship had run its course and they both knew it. What was she to do now?

After Cara started school and didn't need a full-time nanny any longer, Justin had helped in finding a job that she truly enjoyed. And at his suggestion, she had found a wonderful apartment and had just finished moving in the day before. Despite the separation, she hoped the move would awaken their dying relationship. But now that it was abundantly clear he had no interest in furthering the liaison, should she return to North Carolina or should she stay? Resigned, she shook her head. She had some decisions to make.

"Do you mind if I sit with you? From the looks of things, we're both here alone."

Ryan Hamilton had materialized at her side. He had watched the entire exchange between the two, and decided this was his cue to step out of the shadows and formally introduce himself. The fact that Justin and Virginia were supposedly involved, had led him to pause for any sign of discord before moving forward. And after witnessing the indifference from both parties, now was the time. If ever there was a relationship that was finished, it was theirs.

Although Virginia appeared attentive enough to Justin, her body language said otherwise. And that apathetic peck on the forehead spoke volumes as to where Justin's loyalties lied and they certainly weren't with Virginia. The duo's lackluster attachment was inhaling its last breath, so he thought he would take it upon himself to kill it off once and for all.

Ryan had the good fortune to happen upon Virginia a few times around town. He doubted if she noticed. He was always out of her viewing range when he encountered her. The first time he saw her was at a fundraising event for a new community center. He was there to scope out the political climate and competition that was certain to be present. Politicians never missed an opportunity to glad hand with the city's constituents. Even then he could tell that Justin and Virginia weren't as involved and loving as a couple should be. After the pair left the event, he quietly inquired after her and found that indeed she and Justin Graham were an item. Justin was one of his biggest financial supporters. But he vowed if he learned, just for a second, there was a crack in their bond he would take advantage of it. And now it seemed he had found a fissure big enough to run a train through it.

Virginia gazed up at the man's deep, penetrating voice. Its resonance sent tremors through her core, right down to her toes. "No, I don't mind at all." She removed her purse from the empty chair next to her.

After seating himself, Ryan held out his hand for introductions. "Ryan—"

"I know who you are," she cut in. Virginia placed her delicate hand in his masculine one. "How can I not with your face plastered everywhere?" Virginia's smile returned with her introduction. "Virginia Cooke," she offered."

Justin's loss can surely be this man's gain.

Virginia let her gaze casually, but discreetly, roam Ryan's body encased in a well-fitted charcoal gray suit. She didn't let it slip past her that the abstract designs in his tie was nearly the same pale blush color as her dress. The color harmonized perfectly with the tie's gray background. Anyone who saw them together would certainly think they were a couple.

Virginia had done her homework too. Ryan Hamilton was charismatic, rich, handsome *and* single. Rumor had it, he'd come close to marriage once but the woman he loved passed away from a sudden and rare cancer. Reportedly, he was there by her side until the moment she took her last breath. It was said that he could never find anyone to take her place, hence the single status.

Virginia coolly wondered if she had what it would take to be that replacement. It certainly would be fun to try.

"Pleased to meet you Virginia." Ryan raised her hand to his full, seductive lips, never taking his eyes from hers.

Laughing at a joke told by one of the attendees, Justin turned just in time to catch the exchange *and* the welcoming smiles on both their faces.

Chapter 13

Eric watched his bride make her way down the aisle towards him. He was filled to the bream with the joy he held in his heart. Kaitlin Ellis was more than he could have expected from any woman. He felt more than blessed at having her in his life. Before she came along, there had been a few women but none that satisfied his soul the way she did. She was the anchor he had unknowingly been searching for his entire life. With both of his parents gone and no other family, she was all the family he needed. Leaving the love of his life for a second, his gaze swept out over those in attendance. Most of his officers who weren't on duty had joined him to celebrate. He smiled at the men and women who gave him their nods and thumbs up.

He glanced to his left at his best man who was fixated on his soon to be ex-girlfriend, who in turn was ignoring him and smiling up at Ryan Hamilton seated next to her. And from the looks of things, Justin just might have changed his mind about Virginia. Eric mentally shook his head. It's funny how those old sayings were always found to be true. Justin was all set to let her go until he discovered someone else wanted her. Refocusing on his bride, Eric extended his hand once she reached him. Now that he had her, he was never letting her go.

∞

The ceremony was beautiful. They both had decided to recite their own vows and once they were finished, most of the women in attendance had pulled out a tissue or handkerchief. After exchanging rings, the duo gazed lovingly into each other's eyes as the minister proclaimed their sacred union. Honeymoon or not, Eric couldn't wait to make love to his wife.

He had reserved a suite in one of the upscale hotels downtown for their wedding night. Every fantasy KT shared with him concerning this day, he had fulfilled by the staff, which was waiting to satisfy their every whim. They would briefly attend the reception in the elegant ballroom of the estate, before quietly leaving for their mini honeymoon. He left strict instructions with Justin not to let anyone disturb them, including the department. He didn't care if the city was burning down around them. He wanted all of his focus to be on his new bride. He reserved the suite for 2 days and planned not to surface until the very last second was used up.

After they were officially introduced as husband and wife and had turned as one to greet their guests, ear piercing explosions rang out; effectively upsetting the day's joy. It took several seconds for Eric to realize the familiar eruptions he heard were high powered rifle shots. And by the time this horrific fact had registered, a lot of the guests were already in full stampede mode.

Before he could utter a word, KT had slumped into his arms with them both landing on the ground. He covered her with is body while trying to assess what was taking place. Even with the chaos erupting all around them, his senses had focused on the lack of movement from his new spouse, he peered down to find she had been hit. Catching sight of the profusely bleeding wound, he immediately used his hands to cover the gaping hole; trying his best to stop the blood flow. When it was understood he could not, he shouted for help.

People were screaming and running all around them as more shots rang out. The expensively decorated garden was in pandemonium. Not knowing what else to do, Eric continued pressing on the wound and shouting for help. And just as suddenly as the shots started, they abruptly stopped. While Eric held onto his wounded wife, Justin shielded the couple the best he could; grabbing at anyone he could reach to help him keep Eric and KT from being trampled. But the people who ran passed the distressed couple, were too concerned for their own safety to be of any help.

Once the shooting stopped, Dr. Jon Payne instructed his date, Metro Regional Hospital nurse Shelby Kirkland, to retrieve his medical bag from his car. Jon's brother Landon made sure she had safe passage by directing one of the attending officers to escort her. While Shelby retrieved Jon's medical supplies, Jon and Landon pushed their way through the sea of fleeing people; trying to reach the helpless wedding party.

While Jon and Shelby attended to KT, several of the attendees, along with police personnel from Eric's division and others, searched the grounds for the gunman or gunmen. Tor Hudson, KT's good friend and boss, helped search every inch of the estate for the sniper. Although he was fully engaged in his task, his mind was back with Eric and KT.

Who could have done this and why? How could this have happened with the garden filled with so many of Metro City's police force?

He was grateful his own wife was safe at home. If it hadn't been for the flu, Andee would have been right there in the thick of things. He didn't need to be worried about her too. After searching everywhere, he met back up with Kobe who was attending the wedding with Blake. He, like everyone there, had come to celebrate Eric and KT's nuptials, not to become a part of a crime scene.

"Anything?" Tor asked Kobe.

He shook his head. "Nothing and we looked everywhere." Kobe was agitated. Watching Eric cradle a bloody KT, brought back unwanted memories of Bria.

"How the hell did he get away? This place is swarming with cops and no one saw anything?" Tor too was frustrated. This SOB had the balls to shoot a cop's wife while surrounded by police personnel from damn near every division in the city.

"Where is Blake?" Once again thinking of Bria, Kobe found himself suddenly on the edge of panic. He needed to make sure she was out of harm's way. When the shooting started, he pulled Blake to the ground with him and after it was over he instructed her to stay put while he joined the search.

Tor nodded towards the platform. "She's helping Payne with KT."

Blake was helping by trying to calm Eric. He was out of his mind with worry. Tor noted, from the look on Jon's face, Eric had a right to be.

I hope she makes it." Tor caught the doctor's silent exchange with Shelby and read it instantly. Things weren't looking good.

Kobe held sight of Blake rubbing Eric's back in a soothing motion and relaxed. She was okay.

Both men's attention was drawn back to the task at hand, by the arrival of the ambulance. They both ran in the direction of the siren, hoping it wasn't too late.

∞

Virginia was out of breath by the time they made it to Ryan's car. As soon as the first shot rang out, he pushed her to the ground and shielded her with his body. And for one wild moment she wondered if Justin would have taken it upon himself to protect her. But before she could speculate further, there were more gunshots. And with each round, Ryan held her tighter. After it appeared the gunman had fled, he lifter her to her feet and hurried her to his car. He knew they couldn't leave, but he needed to get her out of the gunman's target range.

"Are you alright?" Ryan took a cursory sweep of her shapely body; looking for any signs of trauma. No one was going to hurt her as long as he was there. He would protect her at all cost.

Catching her breath Virginia nodded that she was fine. "Was anyone hurt?" Because of Ryan's quick thinking she hadn't seen KT fall to the ground.

"From what I could see, I think the bride was shot."

Virginia's eyes widened with this news. "Oh no, KT!" She tried to head back to the garden to check on her friend, but Ryan stopped her.

"Virginia No! The gunman could still be on the grounds. Here…" Taking a fob from his pocket, he unlocked the car and placed her in the passenger seat. After tilting the seat backwards, he started the car to allow the air conditioning to do its job so she could rest.

"Stay here while I check on her." Without a thought, he kissed her on the mouth before rushing back to the garden; leaving Virginia to touch the spot where their lips met. In the midst of the chaos, she smiled.

∞

Ryan waded against the throng of people still fleeing the garden. The Valero's had upwards of three hundred guests all fleeing from the crime scene in one direction at once. He was lucky to have gotten Virginia out when he did. He reached the bride and groom just as the ambulance arrived.

"How is she?" He whispered to Justin who had taken over Landon's job of keeping Eric out of Jon's way.

He deliberately kept his voice low, as not to panic Eric who was barely balancing on the edge of reason. Ryan caught the slightly perceptible negative shake of Justin's head. Things weren't good; not good at all.

Although he was concerned for his friends, Justin gave Ryan a few more moments of attention. When the shooting started, the first person he thought of was Virginia. But as he was trying to make a decision to stay put or go after her, he saw Ryan push her to the ground shielding her as the melee continued, causing him to hit the ground for his own safety. By the time he surfaced, he caught sight of Ryan rushing her from the garden.

Justin didn't know how he felt about this development between Ryan and Virginia. He could barely get through the ceremony without stealing glances at the 'new' couple. He didn't know why it bothered him. He and Virginia were over and he had planned to tell her so later that evening. So technically, she was free to see whomever she pleased. What bothered him was the fact that she made the transition before anything was formally agreed upon and so smoothly. Had she and Hamilton been seeing each other before now?

He brought his attention back to KT when the paramedics arrived with their equipment. He and the other's let them have the space with Jon rattling off her vitals and instructions. Justin turned to address Ryan again, but the man was gone. And he knew exactly where he was headed. Back to wherever he had stashed Virginia.

∞

Blake Steele hugged herself while she watched the paramedics move into action. She also kept note of Dr. Payne's worried expression. He didn't think KT was going to make it. Her gaze quickly shot to Eric who was now hyperventilating. He may not have understood all that was going on at the moment, but he had sensed none of it was good. Shelby took over in assisting the EMTs while Jon attended to a panicking Eric.

"Are you okay?" Kobe asked Blake. He gathered her into his protective and comforting embrace. He finally had a moment to properly check up on her.

Blake was on the verge of tears as she shook her head against his chest. She couldn't help her friends. KT was possibly dying and Eric was going through hell watching the medical team work to save his wife's life. She met Eric after her brother was arrested for murder. And shortly after, she was introduced to KT, with the women becoming fast friends.

"Come on. Let me take you home." Kobe kissed the top of her stylishly cut hair before releasing her to lock their fingers. There was no way he was letting her out of his sight until she was safely home.

"If you don't mind, could you take me to the hospital? I want to be there for Eric." Kobe gave her a lopsided smile. She had grown so much since he first met her that day at police headquarters. He nodded.

When Kobe met Blake Steele, she was anything but warm and giving. Although she wasn't as bad as her obnoxious brother, she still welded an air of entitlement, or at least that was his first impression. He soon came to realize her behavior was borne more out of pain and not privilege. She may have had money that had given her a status above most people, but it was the lack of her mother's love that made her come off as cold.

"Come on." Kobe nodded at Tor and Landon as he led Blake to his car to follow the ambulance. He didn't have to worry about her at the hospital. Eric's division would have the place locked down. As soon as he got Blake settled, he was coming back to help with the investigation. They had to find the person responsible for this.

Chapter 14

Ryan took the key from Virginia's still trembling hand and unlocked her apartment door. Even though Justin brought her to the wedding he made sure *he* was the one to bring her home. She may have been stoic during the shooting, but when he returned to his car, he found her doubled over in the seat shaking like a leaf. The danger of the day had caught up to her. After finding her distraught, he immediately pulled her into his arms; soothingly caressing her back and relaying calming words to comfort her worried soul.

Once inside, Virginia motioned to Ryan. "Make yourself at home...I'll be right back." She wanted to change her clothes and compose herself. When Ryan returned with the news of KT's condition, she was already panicked over the chaos. She realized any one of them could have been killed. And if things didn't improve with KT, someone would lose their life. She took her time changing and by the time she was done, she was composed enough to join her guest.

Virginia returned to the common room to find Ryan had opened a bottle of wine and had poured each of them a glass. The bottle was from a case Justin had given her as a housewarming gift. She smiled. He had indeed made himself at home. Ryan had taken off his suit jacket and loosened his tie. He met her with a glass of her favorite Burgundy. He watched her eyes close as she released a slow breath after taking that first taste.

"Feeling better?" He asked after her second sip of the soothing liquid.

She nodded. "Yes I am." Then she shook her head. "I just can't get over what happened to KT. Do they have any idea who shot her or why?" Ryan responded in the negative.

At that moment her empty stomach reminded her she hadn't eaten anything that day. Placing her glass on a tabletop, Virginia smiled through her embarrassment. "How about I cook us up something quick to quiet the rumbles?" She started towards the kitchen and a group of haphazardly marked boxes sitting on the kitchen island. "Just as soon as I find my pots and pans that is. I just finished moving in here yesterday," she continued as she examined an open box.

Retrieving her glass, Ryan followed her into the kitchen. "I hope you don't mind. I took it upon myself to order take out from *Randy's Place*." He checked his watch. "The food should be here soon." Ryan took a taste from his own glass; awaiting her answer.

Virginia stopped hunting for her cookware to raise an eyebrow. The gesture was not lost on Ryan. She was fine with him opening a bottle of wine. She *had* told him to make himself at home, but this? She accepted the outstretched wine glass as she considered the gesture.

Ryan placed his glass on a countertop. From her hesitation, he realized he needed to clear a few things. He had always been a take charge kind of guy, but he also knew he had to be careful of boundaries when it came to women; especially this woman who he was very interested in. He certainly didn't want her to think he was by any means controlling.

"Let me explain. I am not a control freak or anything like that. I just wanted to make the rest of this difficult day a little easier for you. No one could have predicted this would have happened and it is upsetting. My intentions were to ask you to dinner *after* the ceremony, but then all hell broke loose." He watched Virginia visibly relax.

He didn't mean to alarm her; he just wanted her to be comfortable. It had been a trying day for them both. Before they were allowed to leave the estate, each guest had to give statements to the police, who had taken more time then he would have liked. It had taken a lot to calm her enough to tell what she had seen and heard. Virginia was still shaken and exhausted by the time they made it to her home.

"It's fine. But I must tell you, you did give me a start. Mainly because no one had ever done anything like that for me before without asking or being told. And you hear so many stories about stalkers and such." She shrugged and took healthy swallow from her glass.

Virginia usually prided herself on being a good judge of character and although she didn't get any kind of warning bells from Ryan, there was always a first time. But the real reason she was surprised, no man, not even Justin had shown that level of concern for her. The care he'd shown her, from protecting her from the gunman to ordering food, was all new to her. She would like to think Justin would have done the same, but up until that point, he hadn't shown that much consideration. And to further hammer the point home, she hadn't seen or heard from him since the mayhem began. She suddenly realized that her position as Cara's nanny had placed her in a precarious situation as Justin's girlfriend. It was she who made plans and took care of him instead of the gestures being shared. She guessed both of them found it easier. Since she was already caring for his daughter, Virginia had managed to just add him to her list of tasks with him allowing her without any opposition. Justin rarely took the initiative, unless it directly involved him. She marveled that it took the attention of another man to make her aware of what had been missing in her relationship with Justin.

"Well my lady, you don't have to be worried about me becoming a stalker or anything like that. But I will tell you this. When I'm interested in a woman, I go all out in letting her know that. You won't ever have to guess where you stand with me. And if you want to know something just ask. I have nothing to hide. I'm an open book." Ryan spread his arms apart to punctuate his point.

"So are you saying that you're interested in me?" This time she raised a brow with a small, knowing smile. She hoped that was what he was saying.

"Yes." It was as simple as that. He made his intentions known. He was about to ask her how she felt about his declaration, when her doorbell rang.

Virginia placed her glass on the dining table and excused herself, before hurrying off to answer the door. Whoever it was had bad timing. She wanted to explore his answer some more. Expecting the food had arrived, she didn't bother checking the peephole. She opened the door to Justin instead.

"Oh wow, so you did make it home. I was worried when I couldn't find you."

Justin immediately stepped across the threshold when she opened the door; forcing her to step aside. Virginia had every intentions of stopping him from entering, but he had made that impossible. Closing the door behind him, Justin pulled her into a tight embrace before kissing her fully on the lips.

Wide-eyed, Virginia froze. Where was *this* coming from? He all but patted her on the head at the wedding and now he was kissing her like there was no tomorrow? She had her answer when Ryan cleared his throat from somewhere behind them. Justin released her with a smile. But it didn't quite reach his eyes as he stared at Ryan. To Ryan, Justin's smile was more of a sneer.

"Ryan Hamilton, what are you doing here?"

Justin took in Ryan's casual demeanor; the absence of his jacket and the glass of wine—*his wine.* He also noted the loosened tie. The man looked very much at home. As much has it killed him, he continued to smile even though he wanted to slug that confidence right off his smug face.

Ryan shrugged, before lifting the decoratively etched glass to his lips; never taking his eyes from Justin.

Savoring the delightful liquid even more, he finally answered. "I thought I would be a gentleman and make sure Virginia got home safely."

He lifted his glass again; this time to hide his satisfaction. Justin was furious and it pleased him. Ryan was almost certain Justin knew he had brought Virginia home. That's why he was there. But if he thought he would back down just because he showed up, he was sadly mistaken. And no amount of money Justin may have donated to his campaign would be a hindrance either. He would gladly return every cent, if he was petty enough to make it an issue. Justin had lost his claim on Virginia the moment he planted that indifferent lack of affection on her forehead.

"That was gracious of you." Justin nodded his full understanding of the 'kind' gesture, while trying to pull Virginia closer to his side, only to have her pull away.

Turning to Virginia he dismissed Ryan. "Do you think we could talk?"

Ryan kept his mouth shut and continued to enjoy his wine *and* the moment. He was curious as to how this little scenario would play out. He was by no means insecure, but from the looks of things, Justin sure was.

Virginia blinked at his audacity. "Not tonight. As you can see, I have a guest and we're about to have dinner." She couldn't believe him.

Virginia dug in by folding her arms under her generous breasts, pushing the exposed tops of them up and into view. Justin, catching sight of what used to be his threatening to spill free of her button down shirt, was about to insist, when the doorbell chimed again; saving him from Ryan's intervention if he had persisted.

"I'll get that. It's probably our food." Ryan grabbed his wallet from his inside jacket pocket and headed for the door. Not giving either of them a chance to rebuff.

Virginia smiled appreciatively at Ryan before leading Justin into the common room and turning on him. Her eyes narrowed. "Why are you here?" She hissed at him through clenched teeth. "You could have just as easily called to see if I had gotten home. And don't you think for one minute when you suggested that we *talk* at the wedding, that you weren't hinting that it was over between us. I'm not stupid!" She let him know that she was up on his shenanigans with Ryan.

"So yes, to save us both some time, I concur with your decision. We should end this and move on," she continued.

"From the looks of things you have already *moved on*," he countered through a whispered retort of his own.

"From this point on, what I do or not do is none of your business," she volleyed back, just as Ryan returned to the room with the food.

"Justin, I would offer for you to stay for dinner, but I only ordered enough for two," Ryan informed a now visibly irate Justin.

Softening, Virginia answered for him. "Ryan, it's fine. Justin was just leaving." As far as she was concerned, it was past time for him to bow out. She should have ended the derailed mess the moment he ignored her after returning from her visit with her mother.

With one last glance at the expectant duo, Justin turned on his heels and left them to their new relationship.

Chapter 15

All the blood drained from Alec's face as he listened to the special news report.

"Jocelyn, I'm standing amongst the debris resulting from this afternoon's chaos at the infamous Powers' estate. I'm told a gunman or gunmen opened fire striking Kaitlin Ellis Valero, newly wedded wife of decorated police Lieutenant Eric Valero. From what I understand, the couple had just been pronounced man and wife, when the shots rang out and Mrs. Valero was hit. The police do not have a suspect at this time, but they are confident they will get to the bottom of the shooting that took place here earlier today." Charismatic field reporter Ted Calhoun informed his television audience, as well as news anchor Jocelyn Sanders at KWPL, Metro City's popular news channel.

Staying on point, Jocelyn asked her scripted question. "Ted, do we know the extent of Mrs. Valero's injuries at this time?"

"Well, from what I've been told, she is in critical condition at this time Jocelyn. Our thoughts and prayers are with the detective and his new wife. Wishing her a speedy recovery. Back to you Jocelyn."

"Thanks Ted, a speedy recovery indeed. In other news…"

Alec let the new anchor's voice fade into the background. He had heard enough. Even though they didn't have a suspect, he would wager every penny he had that it was his rogue nut job. The man had been dormant for months only to resurface to kill the detective's wife on their wedding day?

Alec broke out in a cold sweat at the implications if this man was caught. He was running on pure revenge which meant he could and would make mistakes that landed him in his grave or in a prison cell. And if the latter happened, he knew for certain he would not hesitate to throw him under the bus just for kicks. There was no doubt that he blamed him for everything. He had to find him before the police did. But how? The man stopped communicating with him months ago. He didn't even know where to begin to look. And even though there was no real proof they were connected, any investigation would tank his bid for mayor for sure. The people of Metro City had seen too many times what city officials were capable of. He would be found guilty in public opinion without an ounce of proof.

Picking up the phone, he replaced it again. He couldn't make this call on a landline. Unlocking his desk drawer he reached for one of two burner phones to place his call. Reluctant to use Owen Meeks, he would have to employ the man's help after all. He may know ways of finding his predecessor than he did. This was beginning to be more than he could deal with. How could a simple plan go so horribly wrong? All he wanted was to be mayor, but the unnecessary body count continued to rise. It was easier when he did all the heavy lifting himself, but he couldn't be everywhere, hence his need to outsource.

Putting the phone down, Alec thought better of involving Meeks. The man knew little of his operation and he needed to keep it that way. He would somehow have to find Santiago on his own. He couldn't risk exposing anymore people to his already out of control plan. He just hoped if the police found Rafe Santiago before he did, they would kill him before he could talk. He pulled another drawer open and retrieved a forty year old bottle of scotch. He had been saving it for after he became mayor, but with the way things were going he needed a few shots to get his nerves under control. If he lost control now, everything he worked so hard for would be lost. After knocking back the first shot, Alec took another. He felt better. He would be mayor of Metro City come hell or high water.

Chapter 16

Rafe took a healthy swallow from his own drink. He
had managed to return to his hideout without incident. He
found himself a secluded cabin in the midst of a piney area
twenty-five miles outside of town. The moment he took on
full time with Alec, he knew he needed a place to hide out
in case things went bad. The eager owner of the place was
more than happy to accept cash. He had been trying to
unload the place for years, but no one wanted to live that
deeply secluded in the woods. Not trusting the man not to
talk, Rafe promptly placed a bullet in the back of the old
guy's skull the moment he turned to count his windfall.
Rafe buried him out back under one of the tall pines on the
property. Because the old man was a loner and had no
family, no one would come looking for him. The location
was a serene spot where he could relax and plan without
interruption. What he had planned took every ounce of his
focus to carry it all off without a hitch, and so far it had
worked.

After he shot up the Valeros' wedding, he took his
time walking back through the wooded area that opened out
into the nearby park. The rifle he used had been broken
down and hidden in a backpack; casually swung over one
shoulder. There weren't many people in the park and the
ones who were there, never saw him. He parked his vehicle
just beyond the edge of the tree line, not hidden but not
easily visible either. Placing the pack in the bed of his
truck, he looked around before sliding into the driver's side
of the stolen pickup. He had 'borrowed' the truck from

police impound days before. No one even knew it was missing.

Rafe had learned the useful trick of hiding vehicles in plain sight when he was a rookie with the department. If you brought in vehicles for impound when the yard was swamped, the attending officer would trust you to log it yourself instead of waiting for him to find time to get around to it. The truck he borrowed was one he had "mistakenly" forgotten to log in. He even had the keys. He thought he would just hold on to them just in case he needed to use it someday; and he had. So when the attendant went to lunch, he just helped himself. And because the man expected to return shortly, he didn't bothered to set the padlock to the gate; a clear violation of policy.

When it was time for him to 'hide' his getaway vehicle, he simply returned it to its rightful place without a worry. With everyone out looking for who shot up the detectives wedding, it was a piece of cake. There wasn't an officer in sight. Besides, none of his former colleagues were looking for him, let alone vehicles from their very own impound lot.

Now he sat on the porch of his cabin downing beers retrieved from a makeshift ice chest, watching news clips of the day's events on his smart phone. The latest update said the new bride was fighting for her life. He hoped the bitch died. He wanted Eric Valero to feel the impact of a destroyed life just as he had.

Rafe twisted the top off another bottle as he relived the feeling of shooting Valero's wife. He purposely waited until they were official before taking the shot. The other shots were just decoys. She was his only target for the evening. He savored the panic and horror that colored his former boss's face. He imagined every expression that played across the surface of Valero's face was what must have resembled his own when he watched himself in that video with that bitch Jess Ashford. All Valero had to do was hold onto the contents of that packet and do nothing and he would have been safe. But he just had to save Landon Payne's ass, his next to the last target.

Landon Payne. Too bad he didn't have a special someone or he would have shot her too. No, when he finally did get around to Payne, it would be a direct hit. He didn't deserve any of the good things that came his way. It was bad enough restaurant owner, Trudy Franklin, left Landon wealthy, but Valero protecting him and making him detective despite him sleeping with that whore Jesse, was just too much. He would have made sure she paid too had she not dropped off the face of the earth. The bitch had good sense to leave town after the scandal she created.

And Alec Campbell. He couldn't wait to wipe that self-satisfying smirk off of his narcissistic face. One down and two more to go. Rafe swallowed the entire contents of the bottle before reaching for another.

Chapter 17

"What do we know so far?" This was from Commander Nedra Scott who had joined the group at the Powers' estate. She had been called to the scene to take over the investigation. Nedra was a twenty-eight year veteran who headed the detective division of the Metro City Police Department.

"From the looks of it, Kaitlin Valero was the only one shot. There were numerous gunshots but no one else was hit," Landon informed her. "We also have concluded from the position of the shots were fired, that it's likely one shooter." After he and some of his colleagues surveyed the area, they concluded there couldn't have been more than one person.

It was early evening with the sun sinking low on the horizon. Powerful spotlights had been placed around the perimeter to aid those investigating the shooting. Several detectives and officers were still combing the grounds for clues; hoping to find anything to solve this puzzle.

Nedra shook her head. "I don't get it. This person got off multiple rounds and managed to only hit Eric's wife? Could she have been the target all along?"

Kobe spoke up. "It looks that way." He and Tor were summoned to be included in the briefing.

The commander turned to Tor. "Hudson, was she working on anything that may have upset someone?"

Tor shook his head. "The only thing she had been working on for the past few weeks was her wedding. She hasn't been in the office at all for nearly two months. She wanted to concentrate on her life with Eric, nothing more." Tor shrugged.

"How is she doing by the way?" Assessing the yard, Nedra shook her head at all the mess that was made by the fleeing guests. She was supposed to be in attendance, but an important call hindered her from making the wedding. She was on her way to join the reception when she got the call.

"We don't know. The last time I checked, she was still in surgery," Tor told her.

"I know from my brother, things didn't look so good before she was transported to Metro Regional. Jon was worried when they loaded her into the ambulance." Landon hoped they were able to save her.

"Ok, any ideas where the shots came from?" Nedra had transitioned to all business.

"From what we could gather, the gunman was hidden along the tree line there, behind the open garden. About twenty yards beyond is an asphalt foot path the residents like to use to get around the neighborhood. The path winds through the woods then leads back to a park about two and a half miles north of here." Landon and some of the officers had discovered it before she arrived.

"And since the path begins at Fulton Lake, which you know has no outlet, it's safe to say, he took the path back to the park. We have some people down there now looking for clues and questioning everyone," Landon concluded.

"Mr. Hudson, West," she addressed Tor and Kobe, "you aren't apart of the department, but I know Lt. Valero has worked closely with your agencies in the past and he trusts you. I have no problem doing the same. We don't have as many detectives as we used to. I know you both understand that's due to the ones who were fired or jailed for being connected to the former mayor's criminal enterprise. So I'm grateful for any help that you can give us on this case. Just keep me informed." Both men nodded.

Nedra gazed at each man individually. Both, along with their colleagues, were highly trained professionals who were more than up to the task. She wished she had more men like Tor and Kobe working for her team. Once, she had even hinted at them joining the force, even though she didn't have much hope of that happening. Both men, exceedingly skilled at their craft, would be fools to leave their lucrative positions. Even top ranking officials within the department didn't make the money those two pulled in.

Nedra drew Landon aside for more instructions, before heading to the hospital to check on Eric and KT.

Kobe shook his head while he and Tor walked the grounds again. "There is no way we could have seen this coming. No way!"

Tor agreed. "For the life of me I can't think of anyone who would have it out for her. There has to be something we're not seeing. Could the gunman been aiming at Eric and hit KT instead?"

"If that was the case, he had plenty of opportunity to take Eric out but he didn't," Kobe reminded him.

"Damn it!" Tor was frustrated. They didn't have a clue as to who was to blame and no leads. Where were they supposed to start?

∞

"Eric, Eric how is she?" Nedra rushed towards him.

It was late evening and Eric was pacing the private family room still covered in his wife's blood. KT's cousin Myka was there with her boyfriend, the former DA turned writer, Garrett Pleasant, along with their friends Cymone Tully and Nate Morrison. They were upstairs visiting Queen when they heard the news.

Eric swiped a hand down his face. "She's still in surgery. Nedra I can't lose her, I just can't."

Nedra pulled an emotional Eric into what she hoped was a comforting embrace. His pain was too great to fix. She felt so bad for them. She had known Eric since he first joined the force and watched him move through the ranks to his present position. She liked him and respected him and his wife. She knew good people when she saw them and did everything she could to assist Eric with his division.

"Eric, Kaitlin is going to make it. I have faith that she will and you must too."

Eric pulled away when he saw Dr. Payne coming towards them. He looked tired but he was smiling. That smile alone brought immediate relief to Eric. It had to be good news.

"Eric, your wife is going to be just fine. She lost a lot of blood, but once we got inside, the damage wasn't as great as we expected. She's in recovery, but as soon as she's move to a room I'll have a nurse let you know." He clasped Eric's shoulder and nodded at the rest of the group before turning to leave the room. Jon was glad he was able to bring them some good news.

Elated, but exhausted himself, Eric stumbled and collapsed. The full weight of the day had finally landed on him. The group shouted after Jon, who rushed to his side. Eric was still conscious, but weak. The strain from the day and the fact that he hadn't taken food or liquids had left him stressed and dehydrated. Jon had Garrett find a nurse and to ask for a gurney. It was time that he took care of the groom.

Dizzy and weak, Eric still managed to smile knowing that his Kaitlin was going to be alright.

***

KT woke to a sleeping Eric. After he was given some food and something to rehydrate him, he wouldn't stop until he was at her bedside. KT found him stretched out on the sofa near her bed with his arms folded, sound asleep. She tried rising but the pain that shot through her prevented the movement. She felt along the bandage that was wrapped around her middle. It took her a few moments to remember what happened. That's when her smile faltered and her gaze shot back to her husband. His being on the sofa dressed in hospital scrubs and not in a bed, meant he wasn't hurt. She released a sigh of grateful relief. She hoped no one else had been hurt. Still drowsy from surgery, she closed her eyes for what she planned for a moment, but fell back to sleep.

∞

Eric stirred at the smallest of sound. When he opened his eyes he blinked. It took him a moment to remember where he was and when it did come to him he sat up in a shot. Briefly rubbing his eyes, he turned towards his wife. KT along with Dr. Payne were smiling at him. It was her melodic humming that roused him from his slumber. Eric swung his feet to the floor and moved towards them.

"You're awake!" He was so grateful to see her smiling face.

"Well, It's about time you woke up," KT told him, before he captured her mouth in a grateful kiss.

"How is she?" Eric asked Jon. He made sure he wasn't dreaming by cupping her lovely face.

"She is healing nicely, I'm happy to report. There will be a scar to which I recommended an excellent plastic surgeon. But your wife says no way. She wants to retain all the memories of your wedding good and bad." Jon shrugged.

"That's my Kaitlin." Eric was more than relieved that she would recover. Now if they could just find the SOB who shot her. Pushing that thought from his mind, Eric leaned in for another kiss from his wife.

Jon took this as his cue to leave. "I will leave you two alone."

He left the newlyweds to their reunion; thankful it was a happy one. Now if he could just get Queen to wake up. She was still in a coma and the longer she remained, the more uncertain he was about her condition. He was still concerned about the swelling that was threatening to take control. He stepped inside her room. Even with the sun shining brightly through the uncovered window, the atmosphere was grim. Syon sat beside her bed staring at her as if he could will her awake. Her closest friend Mika sat in a corner watching them both. The worry on her face was heartbreaking. It was just a year or so ago that the friends were in the reverse situation. Myka had been stabbed and Queen was the one holding vigil, even though they weren't speaking at the time. Just as with KT, Jon had been on the scene when Myka was stabbed on the street after returning to her office during her lunch hour.

"How is everyone?" Jon asked them both. Myka only nodded.

"The question is how is *she* doing?" Meaning Queen. Syon was beside himself. He wanted her to wake up...no he needed her to wake up. He didn't know what he would do if he lost her. So much had been already been taken from them.

"I'm still concerned, but as long as she's stable I am confident everything will be fine. So far we have been able to keep it that way."

Syon nodded. He knew Jon was doing his best for her. As far as he was concerned, there wasn't a better doctor in Metro City. He trusted him completely.

"Have you had your own checkup?" Jon raised a brow anticipating the negative answer he was sure to receive.

"Well..." that was all that Syon could say. He knew he should be taking better care of himself, but he needed Queen to wake up first.

"Here, let me have a look." Jon took a penlight from his pocket and shone it into his eyes. Next he took his stethoscope and listened to his heart. After carefully checking for swelling on his shoulder, he asked Syon about any residual pain in his head. Although Syon tried to down play it, Jon knew from examining his eyes he had some. Syon squinted against the light. Calling for one of the nurses, he instructed pain meds for Syon. He didn't need for him to go down too.

"If the pain persists, I want to run some tests." Syon nodded.

After completing Syon's checkup, Jon checked on his main patient. He shone the same light in Queen's eyes for any sign that she was alert, but found none. He reemphasized the positivity of no swelling and told Syon he expected her to wake anytime. Even as he said it, he prayed that was the case, before leaving the trio to continue his rounds.

Chapter 18

Justin rocked in his expensive leather chair sulking. He had come to the conclusion he had made yet another colossal mistake by letting Virginia go.

What the hell was he thinking? Virginia was the best woman he'd been involved with since Paige. And he really didn't want to revisit the memory on how he messed things up with her. Like it or not, he was reminded each time he saw Paige with her husband. A couple of days before the wedding, he'd overheard Eric congratulating Anderson on expecting their second child. Paige was pregnant again. After learning the great news, the couple chose to be on a beach somewhere celebrating, instead of attending the wedding.

He swiped a hand down his face. Now he was stupid enough to let Virginia go. He tried talking to her again after he was politely dismissed from her apartment, but she firmly stated they had nothing more to talk about. After that, he started seeing her and Ryan together around town. They seemed happy. In fact, Virginia was the happiest he'd ever seen her. She never smiled like that when they were together.

When his daughter asked to see Virginia, this gave him the excuse he needed to try once again to get her to listen to him. He wanted to try to make things work, before she wrote him completely off. And just as they agreed, Virginia came and collected Cara for lunch and an afternoon at the zoo. He offered to tag along, but she declined. After the outing, she returned Cara without actually acknowledging him. Declining again to stay for dinner. Dismissing him a final time, Virginia kissed Cara goodbye and mumbled something about having plans, before dashing back to her car. He had lost her and it wasn't anyone's fault but his own.

"Mr. Graham?" His assistant's voice over the intercom jolted him back to the present; effectively ending his unhappy stroll down memory lane.

Grateful for the reprieve, he pressed the appropriate button to answer her. "Yes Darlene?"

"I have a final check for Mr. Hamilton that needs your signature before I add it to the outgoing mail."

Justin had forgotten all about the money he had pledged towards Ryan's campaign fund. The last check was due tomorrow. He contemplated not paying the last installment, but decided it would be petty to withhold the funds because he'd lost Virginia to the man. It wasn't Ryan's fault he was an ass who pushed her way. He needed to man up and take his lumps and be gracious about it. God forbid he reverted to his old ways and end up in jail, as he had over losing Paige.

"Tell you what, bring me the check and I will deliver it personally." He may have lost Virginia, but he needed to be sure she was in good hands. He would just let Hamilton know he would be there to pick up the pieces, if he didn't treat her right.

∞

Ryan was just about to leave the office for the day when there was a knock at his door. Thinking it was his assistant, he asked the woman to come in. Justin Graham stepped over the threshold instead.

"I was hoping I would catch you before you left. Your assistant wasn't at her desk," Justin explained. He could tell from his expression, he was the last person Ryan expected.

"Justin, what can I do for you?" He met him half way to extend his hand for a shake. Ryan had to hand it to the man; he was being a good sport about losing Virginia. If it were him, he didn't think he would be so polite. But then again, he would never put himself in this position.

"I just wanted to give you my final donation. Man, I'm pulling for you to be our next mayor. You have some good ideas which this city needs, especially after all the past drama."

Ryan smiled. "I just hope the other voters feel the same way. I can see Metro City becoming one of the top cities in the country. It just needs the right guidance at the helm." Ryan accepted the offered envelope and placed it in a lock box for his assistant to deposit in the morning.

"Ryan, I'm just going to say it. I had another reason for personally delivering that check. I wanted to…" Justin sighed. "I wanted to—"

Ryan interrupted him. "You don't have to worry about her Justin. I will take excellent care of Virginia. I'm very fond of her and if I might say, I see a future with her. So there is no need to be concerned." Ryan respected him. He had to admit, he didn't know what to think when he turned to find him standing in his office.

Justin nodded. "I know I messed up and I will be kicking myself for a long time to come. She *is* a good woman who deserves nothing but the best."

"I agree. And I will do everything within my power to make certain she gets the best of all that I can offer her."

Getting what he came for, Justin nodded and left. He could tell that Ryan really did care for Virginia; and if the man's reputation was any indication, she would have the life she deserved.

Chapter 19

Mayoral hopeful Ryan Hamilton frowned. This was not what he expected when he pulled up the voter projections two days before the election. From all intents and purposes, they showed that his opponent, Alec Campbell, was favored to win the mayoral slot by a large margin. Just a few days ago, it was too close to call, but now, it looked as if this race was over.

Closing the web browser Ryan sat back into his chair to consider the possibility of running again in the next cycle. If he did, he would have to come up with a strategy that was sure to place him in that office no matter who was in the race. He had some great ideas to move the city forward to compete internationally, which would put Metro City on everyone's tongue as a positive and bring it out from under the negative headlines of the past. And everyone could agree on how much that was needed. Where most of the previous city leaders concentrated solely on local goals, *his* goals reached beyond the obvious, to bring his city onto a more lucrative social and economic level. The more diverse and forward thinking the city, the more likely corporations were to invest with commerce and jobs; leading to more advantageous opportunities for the citizenry. The city had numerous small businesses that needed the right environment to grow. Presently, Metro City was average. Ryan had a dream to brand it as outstanding.

Although he didn't agree with the city's current thought process, he fully understood it and how it played in his lagging in the polls. The people of Metro City were so weary of the recent crime and corruption, they looked towards anyone whom they could rely on to cleanse their city of its demons. And Alec Campbell's background, as a successful head prosecutor in Elgin, fit the bill. At this point, ridding the city of its negative reputation was foremost in everyone's mind. That aspect he could agree on. But if more jobs and more profitable opportunities were not in place, the undesirable cycle would likely continue. From his observation, both agendas were needed in order to get the city back on track again, and his plan included those elements and more.

He didn't know much about Alec Campbell, other than what was publically known, but as far as he could gather, he only represented one segment of what was needed, nothing more. Alec latched onto the city's hunger to wipe out corruption and ran with it. He didn't need any other platform, because he was promising the only thing the people demanded. But what plans for the city's future did Alec have *after* ridding it of its negative reputation? Ryan didn't think he had any. Which meant the city would continue to be operated in the same matter as its predecessors; leaving Metro City just as stagnant as before.

Deciding to put the election on hold for a moment, he turned his attention to Virginia. They had been seeing each other since the Valero's wedding and he couldn't have been happier. Virginia Cooke was everything he was looking for in a woman; beautiful and smart, with a little bit of sass to make things interesting.

Their first evening together was a pleasant slice of enjoyment. After dinner arrived and they let Justin out, they settled in for a relaxing evening; a great contrast to how the afternoon began. He got to know the woman who had held his attention since the moment he first saw her.

He learned Virginia was an only child to Marvin and Eileen Cooke. The Cooke's had conceived their only daughter late in life, after they had given up on having any children. So overjoyed with their miracle child, the couple gave her all the love and attention she could have ever needed. Naturally smart, he discovered that Virginia parents had raked and saved every penny to send her to college, but it still hadn't been enough. She ended up dropping out at the end of her sophomore year to take a job as a nanny. She was hoping to save enough to return to finish her degree, but things didn't quite work out the way she planned. He learned it was when she took the position with the Grahams, to care for their daughter Cara that she met Justin.

Justin Graham. Ryan shook his head in wonderment. In business, Justin was head and shoulders above the average entrepreneur, but outside of that, when it came to his personal life, Ryan thought the man was an imbecile. How does any man in his right mind allow two good women to get away?

Ryan recalled the circumstances and scandal of Justin's marriage to wealthy socialite, Anastasia Stanton. Justin had screwed over his then girlfriend Paige Bennett, by sleeping with Anastasia for financial gain and getting her pregnant, hence the shotgun marriage. Now here he was again, letting another one slip away. But he was mighty glad he chose to be a fool with Virginia.

Ryan knew all about good women. His former fiancé was one of those jewels. Tragically Gabriella passed before they were able to make a life together. There wasn't a day that went by that he didn't think of her. After she passed, he didn't think he could find another woman who would grab his attention the way Gabby had. With time, the pain of losing her began to diminish, but the loneliness did not. Over the years he tried dating, but the women he saw were selfish and shallow. They wanted to be with him because of what they thought they could gain from him, instead of winning his heart. Now he knew the reason none of the others made the cut. It was because he was waiting for Virginia.

Ryan Hamilton, founder and CEO of Hamilton Enterprises, was one of the top business owners in Metro City. His corporation housed subsidiaries that branched out from construction to manufacturing high end private jets. Ryan moved his headquarters to Metro City after his fiancé's death. He needed a fresh start to put some distance between him and those old heart wrenching memories. Although his business acquired him a ton of wealth, Ryan's life style wasn't over the top. He had nice things, but he never allowed his financial status to be a major factor in his life. For him, it wasn't about the abundance of money or things, it was about the people. He wanted everyone he came in contact with to share in the same opportunities as he had. That was why he wanted to become mayor; to help that process along.

Remembering Virginia's birthday, he retrieved his mobile phone to place an order with his favorite florist. He knew just the thing to add some color to Virginia's day tomorrow. It was time he started spoiling his new lady.

Chapter 20

Virginia smiled when she returned from lunch to find a huge bouquet of hybrid purple Calla Lilies beautifully arranged in a crystal vase sitting on her desk. There had to be at least fifty long stemmed flowers in the expensive hand-crafted vase. She didn't have to read the card to know who they were from. In the course of their intimate conversations, covering many topics, her favorite flowers were mentioned. Virginia grinned when she read the card.

> *"I hope your day is as lovely as these flowers. A beautiful bouquet, for a beautiful lady."*
>
> *R*

She couldn't believe her luck! And he remembered her birthday! Virginia would never have thought the day her relationship ended with Justin would bring a man like Ryan Hamilton into her life. Ryan was fun, attentive and it didn't hurt that he was handsome. She hugged the card to her chest before extracting one of the perfect lilies from the arrangement. She placed the soft petal to her nose. Ryan was like a dream come true that she didn't know she craved. She couldn't help but to compare him to Justin. Ryan's attention highlighted everything that was wrong with her relationship with Justin. With Justin, they rarely ate out without Cara in tow, and when they were without her, the meal was usually a part of some event they attended together. She understood she was Cara's nanny, but at the same time she was also Justin's girlfriend. Looking back, it was as if Justin used Cara as a buffer against growing any real feelings for her. As long as he saw her as the nanny, she was the help and Virginia felt that was all she would ever be to Justin.

When they were together, most of their conversations were centered on Cara, never much about the two of them. But with Ryan, she was treated as a woman whom he was very much interested in. Their conversations focused on either her or them as a couple. He placed no one else between them, not even himself. Ryan made it easy. There was no question that was too personal for him. When she asked about the rumored fiancé, he gladly shared their relationship as well as the circumstances surrounding her illness and subsequent death. And although he made it plain that he loved Gabby, he assured Virginia that Gabby's memory would not interfere with their relationship. He explained that he was all in when it came to the two of them together.

She liked and appreciated Ryan's candidness. He didn't leave her hanging or assuming. He said what was on his mind and encouraged her to do the same. She found this refreshing. From their first evening together, she understood he was there to court her as his and not date her as some miscellaneous, prospective option. Ryan explained he never wasted time when it came to his heart and his heart said he needed her in his life. Virginia felt as if she were dreaming. A man as cultured and established as Ryan Hamilton wanted her!

"Well now. Somebody *really* likes you." This was from Camille Hartley; one of Virginia's coworkers.

Camille resentfully sucked her teeth before plucking one of the lilies from its pricey holder and twirled it between her expensively pampered fingers tips. Jealously eyeing Virginia over the top of the fragrant flower, she brought it to her nose for a healthy sniff.

Virginia tried not to frown at the woman's audaciousness. Among other things, Camille was the office gossip and head troublemaker. She would bet dollars to doughnuts not only was she present when the flowers arrived, but she wouldn't have put it past her to have read the card as well. She made a mental note to see if the envelope had been tampered with once nosey Camille left her cubicle.

"So, who did you have to sleep with to get this kind of money spent on you?" Camille, still holding the flower, cynically eyed Virginia; fully expecting an answer.

Appalled, Virginia considered snatching the lily from her, but quickly reconsidered. She didn't want to touch anything that had been handled by the awful woman. Not only was she a gossip and a troublemaker, she was also the office floozy. Virginia had heard all about Camille's escapades the moment she started working there.

"Sorry to disappoint, but these were sent for a lovely dinner last night. Some of us are appreciated for just our company." Virginia gave the hateful woman a knowing smirk, hoping it would send her on her way. She didn't dare tell the woman the flowers were in recognition of her birthday. The woman already knew too much of everyone's business.

Camille eyed Virginia a while longer before sucking her teeth again and moving on to her workspace, taking the lily with her. Virginia reasoned, with the woman's attitude and reputation, it was likely the only flower of any kind she would ever receive.

Placing her purse in a desk drawer and locking it, Virginia settled in her chair to get some work done. She wanted to finish the claim she was working on so she could leave work on time. She and Ryan had plans.

Because Camille was hidden behind the high walled cubicle, Virginia couldn't see her roll her eyes, before ripping the delicate flower to shreds and tossing the pieces into the trash. Camille was jealous of the new girl. Virginia was attractive and carried herself like a lady, something Camille knew nothing about. She could pretend with the best of them, but her false moral values and modesty always gave her away sooner rather than later. After trying those unnatural attributes on for a short time, lately she didn't even bother to drag them out. It took up too much effort and time to pretend to be something she was not, but at the same time, she wanted the life and respect that came with them. Didn't she?

And that crack about not having to sleep with a man to get flowers hit home and unsettled her. No one ever sent her anything; not a flower, card, nothing, unless she applied pressure for them to do so. Those 'personal' gestures were never borne out of fondness, but were used as tools to disengage, after her 'friends' had become bored with her. When Valentine's Day rolled around, it always found Camille holed up in her workspace seething, as the other women in the office received their anticipated roses and chocolates. Not one of her suitors bothered to even call her. They were busily wining and dining their *real* girlfriends. And this bitch, out of the blue, receives hundreds of dollars' worth of flowers for just having dinner? She was certainly doing *something* wrong. She deserved that type of life. Didn't she?

Camille Hartley wasn't unattractive, in fact she was quite stunning and she knew it. She was five ten, with a generously proportioned figure, which she showed off proudly via the tailored designer clothes she wore that followed flawlessly over every curve. Her even toned, deep chocolate skin glowed with health. Her nails, makeup and costly weave were impeccable, with never a strand of hair out of place. Camille turned heads everywhere she went. Unfortunately, she also used her physical attributes to turn the heads of men—the wrong men, for the wrong reasons.

Everyone within the company knew Camille with most of the women loathing her and most of the men partaking in her readily offered treats. When she wasn't at her desk working, she could be found most times leaning over some man's desk; giving him an eyeful of what mostly likely he had already sampled. If the rumors were true, Camille had slept with most of the men in the building, single *and* married. And the only reason she hadn't rapidly slept her way to the top was due to their boss Anne Peters, who was a sixty year old woman. But most were willing to bet, if there was anything to be gained by it, Camille would have made a run at Anne too.

The only reason Anne tolerated Camille and hadn't dismissed her, was because Camille was good at her job; producing twice the profits than any of her coworkers. In spite of not sleeping with the boss, Anne had promoted her to division director, effective in a couple of days. The current director was retiring and leaving at the end of the week. Despite the fact she was finally moving up within the company *and* would be snagging the coveted corner office, along with lucrative stock options, Camille was miserable. Although she had many acquaintances, she had no real friends. There wasn't anyone with whom she could celebrate her big promotion. Most of the women she knew couldn't stand her. She tried calling a few of her companions, only to have the calls go straight to voicemail. She hadn't bothered to leave a message. An unanswered call usually meant the man in question was done with her.

Camille plopped down in her own chair to try and sort out this new development. When Virginia first started with the company, she tried being friendly, hoping to get some intimate information about her new coworker, but Virginia didn't bite. She was nice enough, but she never wanted to hang after work or have girl talk over lunch. She had overheard one of her fellow gossips on the second floor say Virginia had suddenly lost her last job *and* her man, before landing there. Through the grapevine, she learned Virginia's former employer was Justin Graham of Graham Inc. She gleaned this tidbit of dirt from one of Justin's equally envious employees. According to the gossip, Virginia Cooke was the rich, handsome mogul's live-in bed warmer, until he got tired of her and booted her out into the street.

After discovering this, Camille thought she had found a kindred soul in Virginia, until the uppity bitch started shunning her like she was better than she. And now it seemed the bitch had landed on her feet and latched onto another benefactor. She didn't care what Virginia said, a man didn't pay out that kind of cash for flowers unless she was putting out. Virginia had to be lying.

Having decided Virginia was indeed a liar, Camille consoled her bruised ego with this last thought, before digging into her own work. Whatever the deal with Ms. Virginia Cooke, she was going to do some investigating to find out just what the wanna-be classy thot was doing to get those flowers. With her plan set, Camille directed her attention to the client she needed to contact. She would deal with Virginia later.

Chapter 21

Alec Campbell popped the cork on a very expensive bottle of champagne and poured everyone who was within reach a foaming glass. He did it! The votes had been counted and he was Metro City's new mayor.

After all he had endured, to accomplish the feat, it was well worth the outcome. He looked out over his crowd of supporters and well-wishers as the growing mass chanted his name. Victory couldn't have felt any sweeter. After taking a huge gulp of the flavorful, golden liquid, he handed his glass to his campaign manager. It was time to give his victory address; the speech he had skillfully written and perfected months ago for this very moment. With the crowd going crazy, he had to wait several seconds before the melee died down enough for him to be heard. His people were excited and he couldn't blame them.

"Citizens of this great city, I want to thank all of you for supporting me and believing in me. With your continued support, we will make Metro City the city it should be; a city of greatness and respectability. After tonight, we as a team will bring the crime and corruption to a halt; building a new image of a city you can be proud of again!"

The crowd roared!

Turning towards his election staff, he continued. "I want to give special thanks to my election team. Without any of you, I would not be standing here right now." Alec grinned while vigorously clapping to show his appreciation.

This was all for show. *He* was the real MVP in winning this election.

Each of the staff waved an uplifted hand at the crowd, as their acknowledgement of their boss's accolades. The crowd's roar grew as Alec lifted his own fist into the air before turning again to the group of people who stood next to him. He hugged and shook the hands of his team in victory, while the crowd applauded them all. Even as he accredited his election team, his pride continued to swell from the real drive behind his winning. If it had not been for his careful planning and plotting, not only would his worthy opponent be celebrating instead of him, but he would likely be the major negative topic of the evening news cycle.

With arrogant glee, Alec marveled at the ignorance of the crowd who cheered him. Deciding he alone deserved the praise, he threw out the rest of the speech. He won and that was all that mattered; not even the people who sang his praises.

If they only knew what it had taken to get here.

Alec Campbell returned to the podium to sneer at the unsuspecting crowd with solid arrogance.

He deserved it all.

∞

Across town, at Hamilton campaign headquarters, there was little fanfare. Disappointed, the staff haphazardly started rolled out the catered fare for Ryan's supporters.

Although the staff and attendees tried to put on a good front for their candidate, Ryan's team was visibly saddened. And despite the fact he lost, Ryan didn't let the moment pass without greeting the people who supported him every step of the way.

"Ladies and gents, I want to thank you all for the hard work and dedication you have given to this campaign. Our losing tonight is no reflection on your perseverance. We all fought a good fight and I am eternally grateful for each and every one of you. In spite of the loss, I've decided I will be throwing my hat in the ring in the next election and next time we will win! Now I want everyone to lift your spirits and have a great time!"

The crowd's mood lifted at the announcement he would run again. Win or lose, they would celebrate. Everyone in the room had worked hard and deserved a night of fun. The crowd of people cheered, as he toasted his staff and many supporters. They believed in him. Without them he wouldn't have had a fighting chance. He owed them a lot.

After taking a sip from his champagne glass, Ryan clasped hands with Virginia; pulling her closer to him. He may have been disappointed, but having her there by his side helped ease the sting of losing.

"You are a good man Ryan Hamilton and you should have won this thing *this* time. I don't know much about Alec Campbell, but I do know he can't hold a candle to you. It's a pity more people couldn't see that."

Taking both of their glasses and placing them the podium, Ryan pulled Virginia into a passionate embrace, for a long lingering kiss amid cheers and cat calls from the crowd. He didn't care who saw them, he had fallen for this woman and wanted the whole world to know it. And one of the people who now knew they were together was Camille Hartley.

When she arrived at Ryan's campaign headquarters, her curiosity was piqued when she spotted Virginia in the crowd. But when she saw her at Ryan's side, while he made his speech, her jaw dropped.

"They can't be together. They just can't be," Camille whispered. Even though she tried to rationalize Virginia's presence, all hope was lost the moment Ryan kissed her. Ryan Hamilton was the 'R' who sent Virginia the expensive flowers. Camille ground her teeth, before pushing her way through the crowd to reach the amorous couple.

Not taking her eyes from the two, Camille's indignation grew with each determined step. Virginia was sleeping with Ryan; *her* Ryan. When she finally pushed her way on stage, she impatiently tapped Ryan on the shoulder to stop the madness. Reluctant to end the moment with Virginia, he broke off the affection to turn towards the intrusion.

Irritated, Ryan addressed the unwelcomed intruder. "Camille, what are you doing here?" Ryan hadn't seen Gabby's sister since her funeral a few years ago, and he had hoped to keep it that way.

"Well, I see you've found a replacement for my sister." Camille angrily eyed Ryan, then Virginia. Her outburst was met with an annoyed sigh from Ryan.

"Ryan?" Virginia's question was laced with suspicious wonder. She trusted Ryan, but Camille was a different story.

Virginia thought Camille Hartley would be the last person she would see tonight. She didn't think the woman was savvy enough to be involved in politics or anything else that didn't involve a man whom she could crawl into bed with. Surely Ryan hadn't been involved with the likes of Camille. But what was this about a replacement for her sister?

Ryan stared at Camille while he addressed Virginia's concern. The woman was beyond aggravating. "Virginia, this is Camille Hartley, Gabby's sister."

Camille waved away the introduction. "Virginia knows me, we work together…but it doesn't explain why *you* are with *her*." Frowning, Camille folded her arms; firmly planting herself to await an answer.

"Not that I owe you or anyone else an explanation Camille, but Gabby's gone and I am free to see whomever I like." Ryan eyed the hateful woman with equal contempt. He thought he had made himself clear the last time he encountered her.

"Ryan, you don't know anything about this woman. For all you know she could be some floozy that's after your money. You dishonor my sister's good name by hooking up with the first tramp that seems genuine? My sister was a beautiful soul, but this…" Camille off-handedly flung a hand at Virginia as if she was addressing trash.

Ryan's ire rose with each syllable of Camille's outrageous rant. It was the sudden burst of louder than necessary music that kept him outwardly calm. It also hadn't escaped him the DJ must have predicted Camille's intentions the moment she interrupted them. As if on cue, the young woman had dimmed the lights before hyping the party for the crowd. The attendees weren't even aware of the drama unfolding just below the music's fevered pitch. Ryan caught the young woman's eye and nodded his thanks. He would reward her later. While his supporters shook themselves out of their solemn mood, and began to enjoy themselves, Ryan took Camille firmly by an arm and Virginia tenderly by a hand, and led both women into an empty office; firmly closing the door against any prying ears or eyes.

"Camille, you don't want to go there with me right now," Ryan warned.

"But you don't know anything about her. Who is she really? Does she have the standards of my sister?" Camille's eyes narrowed at a taken aback Virginia. It infuriated her even more that Ryan hadn't released Virginia's hand.

Virginia chose to stay quite against the dig. Any other time she would have defended herself. But it was clear Ryan held the reins to this runaway excuse of a woman.

"You mean, does she have *your* reputation?" Ryan had had enough. Camille had gone too far with her vicious attack against Virginia. He knew bringing up her reputation would put a stop to her nonsense. He also knew she wasn't aware he knew of her dirty dealings.

Camille tore her eyes from Virginia to settle them on Ryan. She studied him as if she had never seen him before. As much as she thought she had kept her extra-curricular activities on the low, it seemed she hadn't covered them well enough.

What does he know?

As if reading her thoughts, Ryan continued. "Yes Camille, I know all about your whorish ways. Did you *really* think I would fall into your bed after Gabby died? Did you? I did my best to let you down gently, after you shamelessly threw yourself at me during your sister's funeral. And again after showing up at my home uninvited, wearing nothing under that rather expensive coat, which I'm sure you blackmailed one of your many lovers into purchasing for you."

With each stinging word, Virginia's eyes were more than opened to *this* Camille. She thought she had the complete rundown on her, but this news was a more complete version.

"I had every intention of never mentioning those sexual plays for my attention. In fact, I had completely erased them from my mind, until you came here setting your tongue against the woman I love."

Camille's horror was twofold. The Ryan she knew would have never brought up old indiscretions; especially not in front of other people. She wouldn't even look at Virginia; she couldn't. Her humiliation would not allow it. But the declaration of his love for Virginia was indeed the last crushing blow to her ego.

With her degradation complete, Camille turned on her heels and tore from the room, with both Ryan and Virginia looking after her. Virginia was in stunned awe at the audacity of the woman.

"Baby, I'm sorry. I don't usually go off like that, but the woman irritates me to no end and with the disappointment of the election and all—"

Virginia stopped his apology with her mouth on his. She heard everything he said, but the part that got her most attention was him loving her.

∞

Camille was in such a hurry to get away from the convention hall, she nearly snatched the handle off of her newly purchased Jaguar coupe; a gift to herself in celebration of her promotion. Once she slid behind the wheel, she hyperventilated. She couldn't believe how Ryan tore into her. If she ever thought she still had a chance with him, his response tonight killed the notion for good.

Yes, she cozied up to him after her sister's funeral. She wanted to comfort him. The gentleman that he was, Ryan carefully rebuffed her. Camille thought it was because they had just buried Gabby; that it may have been too soon. She had always wanted Ryan. She was the one who saw him first at a party she and Gabby had attended together. But instead of falling at her feet, Ryan took an immediate interest in Gabrielle. Camille could only watch them from the sidelines as they both fell in love with each other. She loved her sister, but she thought she was the one who should have had Ryan.

And when Gabby became ill and it was understood that she would not recover, Camille thought she would finally have her chance. After Gabby became bedridden, Camille made sure she was at her bedside anytime Ryan was present, which was a majority of the time. She thought she and Ryan had gotten close during the late night meals they shared when they took a break from Gabby's vigil. And when Gabby finally succumbed to her illness, Ryan had held her close in his arms, while she grieved her sister.

But after some time had passed, she made the foolish mistake of showing up at his home to be comforted properly. Yes, she was nude under her expensive fur, which *she* purchased for herself. She thought it was the right time to show Ryan how much she cared for him. She wanted to make him forget about Gabby altogether, by rocking him gently within her body. But Ryan rebuffed her then too.

She didn't know what she was thinking, charging towards him and Virginia the way she had. But seeing the object of her affection kissing another woman—kissing that woman—made her lose all reasoning and she paid dearly for it. The shame she felt at the disclosure that Ryan knew *all* her secrets was the catalyst needed to wake her up. She finally understood he would never want her; not with all she had done. He saw her as the whore she had sadly become.

Tears streamed down Camille's, meticulously made up face. It wasn't so much that Ryan rejected her and front of Virginia, but that he knew about the men she'd slept with. How could she have believed those men who joined her in her bed wouldn't have talked? Metro City was huge, but she failed to remember the small circles entrepreneurs traveled in. Tonight she found out the hard way just how tight those circles were.

Wiping at her cheeks, with perfectly manicured fingertips, Camille started her car and drove home. It was time she packed up her toys and put her house in order.

Chapter 22

Jimi Leigh couldn't believe her luck. She had been looking all over for him. She spotted Rafe climbing into his car when she was about to drive up to the ATM for lunch cash. With the lunch forgotten, Jimi followed Rafe Santiago from the bank's parking lot.

After the attack at the wedding, Jimi was just as puzzled as everyone else as to who wanted to harm the detective or his wife. Although her initial assignment was tailing Shelby Kirkland, she had taken some time off during the ceremony. She didn't see the need, since the place would be crawling with cops. Who in their right mind would even think to bring gunfire to a policeman's wedding, but there it was. Even her client was stumped with this one. Whatever the motive behind the shooting, it had to involve the Valeros directly.

Discovering Kaitlin Valero had no real enemies that left her husband Eric. Jimi needed to find out as much as she could about Lt. Eric Valero. Once again making another trip to police headquarters, she learned quite a bit. While chatting up one of the rookies, she learned Valero was popular with the division. When asked about anyone reprimanded or leaving suddenly, only two names came up. One officer had left a few weeks prior to the wedding, due to health issues and the other was fired. She now had new information in this particular theory of there being a grudge against the lieutenant. Even though Santiago's firing was handed down by the brass, it was Valero who had the displeasure of telling Rafe he was finished with MCPD for good, when the man showed up—hat in hand—to ask for his job back. After learning this, Jimi wanted to follow up with Rafe, but had been unable to locate him—until now.

Concerning Rafe's firing, Jimi now had what appeared to be the entire story, but she felt there had to be more; even though her benefactor didn't see much use in what was considered a dead lead. As far as her employer was concerned, Rafe Santiago was a nonfactor in any of this. Ignoring her employer's suggestion, on a hunch, Jimi started digging into Santiago's background anyway. She would hate for something else to pop off because she hadn't been thorough. But once she locked onto investigating Rafe, she couldn't find him. With each lead of his whereabouts running into a dead end, the more she intrigued she became.

There had to be something or someone that could lead her too his location. When she visited his home, a helpful neighbor told her she hadn't seen the former police officer since his wife left months ago. Why would Santiago leave his home like that? Especially since the bills and mortgage was still being paid. No one seemed to know where he was, not even his estranged wife, who could have cared less. After learning Rafe had dropped from the radar, she was grateful she ignored her boss's decision of dismissing him. Something wasn't quite right there and she was determined to find out what that was. Just when she was stumped as to where to look next, there he was; leaving the bank's parking lot. Now that she had him in sight she wasn't about to lose him.

∞

Puzzled, Jimi followed Rafe, as he circled the police precinct a couple of times before he fell in line a few cars behind Landon Payne! She'd spotted Landon getting into his vehicle, but had no idea he was Rafe's target until the man pulled away from the curb to follow him.

"Huh?" Jimi didn't know what to make of this. Why was he following Payne? Not having a good feeling about any of this, Jimi continued on with her surveillance.

The three car caravan led to *Randy's Place;* the restaurant Landon owned. With the parking lot completely full and parking on both sides of the street taken near the diner, Jimi passively noted Landon was doing alright for himself. But because the lot was full, Landon was forced to park on a side street a block away. Sticking with her original tail, Jimi followed Rafe two blocks up, where he pulled into an alley. Not wanting to blow her cover, she drove passed him and parked in a convenience store lot a few yards away. She watched Rafe exit the vehicle and take a duffle bag from the trunk; slinging the weighted bag over his shoulder, before heading up the alley towards *Randy's Place.*

"No, no, no…this is NOT good." This new turn of events left Jimi's senses on high alert.

Working quickly, she retrieved her firearm from its hiding place underneath her seat and placed it in her waistband at the small of her back, before donning a light jacket to cover it. She exited her car and followed Rafe up and across the street to the back of an abandoned building, directly across from where Landon parked. She quickly peered around the building just in time to catch Rafe forcing a nailed on board from a doorway. Once the board was removed, he went inside. The more bizarre Rafe's movements, the more Jimi's alarm sounded. Now it was about to explode.

Cautiously she stepped inside the dimly lit area. She could hear water dripping somewhere from deep inside the dilapidated building. The place was a wreck and in her opinion, should have been torn down eons ago. There was a metal staircase to her left. The steps were covered with a thick layer of dust and grime, except for the recent footprints left by Rafe. She quietly followed the footprints to the top floor of the building where she found Rafe setting up a rife on a tripod. She quietly but swiftly moved in behind him. He was so confident that no one knew of his plans, it never occurred to him he was being followed. Just as he was looking down the scope to pull the trigger, Jimi pressed her 9mm just behind his right ear.

"Nope." Jimi made sure he knew he was not alone and that she was there to do business if necessary.

Rafe froze, just before Jimi smacked him across the head with the butt of her gun; knocking him out cold.

With Rafe slumped in a heap on the floor, Jimi grinned at her handy work. But the victory of accomplishment was short lived when she peered across the street and saw Landon Payne's SUV pull away from the curb with him never realizing she just saved his life.

∞

When a handcuffed Rafe came to, he was surrounded by several people in official windbreakers milling around the old factory's top floor, along with a couple of paramedics, who were attending to the cut on his head. The cut wasn't deep; the hard knock was just enough to render him unconscious, nothing more. While he was out, Jimi phoned her benefactor for further instructions, hence the federal agents.

Defiant and annoyed, Rafe said nothing as he was read his rights and led away. Satisfied that she probably solved the mystery of who shot Payne, now she needed to know why. She hoped Rafe was in a talkative mood to clarify the situation. From her investigation, she was led to believe Rafe and Landon were friends. And if this was so, what changed?

Wanting more and more to get to the bottom of this mystery, she followed the U.S. Marshals back to their headquarters where she was to meet with her boss. Her mind was racing. Rafe was using a high powered rifle and it was concluded that the person who shot Detective Valero's wife had used the same. Are the two cases related?

Jimi was willing to bet her life on it. She made a mental note to use this new revelation as leverage, if Rafe Santiago decided not to talk. Maybe if he thought they had already pinned Mrs. Valero's murder attempt on him, he may give it all up.

Jimi smiled. She loved her job.

Chapter 23

Jess Ashford started at the man who was her former driver and bodyguard. Out of all the things she could have guessed about him, a killer was not one of them.

She arrived at the city's Federal Building which housed the U.S. Marshal Service, along with the district's FBI offices, just as Rafe Santiago was being brought in. After Jimi contacted her, she called the Marshals to pick Rafe up. With his previous occupation as a member of MCPD, she didn't trust there not to be more compromised personnel. She could have had the FBI to handle it all, but decided to call in a favor from the Marshals. She didn't have any immoral connections there. She couldn't say the same about the bureau. Following Craven Wallace's criminal reign, every agency was on high alert when it came to anything involving the city's police department. After Metro City's former mayor's arrest, several officers were rounded up as his paid accomplices. So despite her tainted history, Jess still had friends among the feds who were more than happy to assist her.

"Rafe?" Jess didn't know what else to say. She liked him. He was a good officer and family man. And although she inadvertently had a hand in his firing, she felt bad about that. She never wanted anyone who participated in her escapades to get hurt.

Before Jess strolled into the interrogation room, Rafe believed his capture had been orchestrated by Alec Campbell; his way of putting an end to his reign of terror, so to speak. Who else could have guessed what he was up to? Not in a million years would he have thought Jess was behind his arrest. With a humorless smirk, he had to acknowledge the irony of it all.

Rafe stared back at the woman who single handedly ruined his life. Irrationally dismissing his own consenting participation, he wouldn't allow himself to accept his part in the whole mess. He refused to own up to his infidelity as the source of his troubles, when all he had to do was keep his fly zipped and he wouldn't have been involved at all.

Jess cleared her throat and started again. "Why did you shoot Kaitlin Valero?"

The question completely gathered his attention. He fully expected her to lead with his attempt to kill Landon Payne, considering he was literally caught in the act. Her unexpected inquiry threw him. Rafe's already ridged posture stiffened. They knew about Kaitlin Valero. What else did they know?

He paused before he answered; letting his wheels turn a little longer. He was calculating the odds of not spending the rest of his life in prison, but he quickly came to the conclusion they weren't in his favor no matter what he said; even with all he knew.

Shifting in his chair he finally spoke. "What I did concerning Landon and the Valeros, it was all about you."

It was Jess's turn to be surprised. "How the hell is your shooting two people have to do with me?" She couldn't even fathom how she fit into this equation. Even if he felt she had spurned him in anyway, it didn't make sense that he tried to kill two people. She was more than confused.

Rafe blinked at her genuine confusion. In his twisted mind it all made perfect sense. If she hadn't been such a whore, none of this would have happened. If she had only had an affair with him things would have gone quite differently. Even if they had been caught, he would have probably gotten a slap on the wrist and kept his job. But since she had bedded half the earth, the brass couldn't let his indiscretion slide. He would never accept the fact that his on duty infidelity was what got him dismissed from MCPD. In his world, nothing was his fault.

He voiced what he was thinking. "If you hadn't been such a whore, Campbell wouldn't have had anything on you to expose. All of those men; all of those photos and videos." Rafe shook with rage; this time at Alec Campbell. If he hadn't saw fit to send that package to Valero, none of this would be happening.

Jess, who had been casually slumped in her chair, sat ramrod straight at the mention of Campbell. The only Campbell she knew was Alec Campbell and if that was who he was talking about, how the hell did he fit into any of this?

"What Campbell are you talking about?" She leaned in for his response.

Rafe didn't hesitate to answer. "You know…the guy you used to work under in Elgin, Alec Campbell."

Jess's jaw dropped. She hadn't thought about her former boss since she resigned from his office. *What the hell was really going on here?*

Resigned to accepting she didn't know anything at this point, needed clarification. "Maybe you should start from the beginning, because I am not following any of this." Jess leaned back into her chair. This was a tale that was begging to be told and Rafe was chomping at the bit to tell it. She could see it in his eyes. His hatred for her was now overshadowed by that of her former boss.

Rafe grinned. Only too happy to share with her every gory detail; even the things she didn't know about. If he was going down, he was certainly taking the new mayor with him. That bastard may have won the election, but he certainly wouldn't be spending a day in that office; not after he was through. Yeah, Campbell thought he had won, but he was about to prove otherwise.

He fixed his gaze over Jess's left shoulder at the two-way mirror, where he was certain several branches of law enforcement was watching, and spoke to the unseen assembled crowd. That crowd included Jess's curious hire, Jimi Leigh Wilson.

"If you aren't already, you might want to record this," he shouted. To Jess, "*you* might want to kick off your thousand dollar pumps and get comfortable, because what I have to say will take some time, but will be well worth every minute."

Taking his own advice, Rafe relaxed. This would be a saga for the ages. As he began his tale, he shifted the blame to its rightful owner; the one person whom he should have been focused on all along. He could see that now. That bastard Campbell was the true culprit. He should never have sent that package to Valero. He may not be able to kill him, but taking him down was a much better prize. Alec Campbell would experience losing everything just as he had.

Elation crept into Rafe's voice with every sentence. The thought of Alec Campbell's public shame increased it even more. He gladly explained his part in the vile plan and how and why Alec Campbell was behind it all. He also gave up Sgt. Meeks, who neither Meeks nor Campbell were aware he knew about. Rafe assumed a man like Alec Campbell always had a backup plan, so there was no way he was his only flunky. And he was right when he stumbled up on Meeks' dirty dealings.

∞

Jess's head was spinning after the hours long interview with Rafe Santiago. The group had to stop several times to fact check as well as catch a breather from what they had learned. There had been more going on than any of them could have possibly known. Who could have guessed the seemingly unconnected mishaps all led back to her former boss and now newly elected mayor, Alec Campbell? And after learning yet another dirty cop resided inside the Metro City police department, Jess was correct in not letting them in on the arrest of Rafe Santiago. It would be easy for Sgt. Meeks to skip town after being named in this latest duplicity; not to mention possibly tipping off his boss of his coming arrest. Now they had the opportunity to catch them both by surprise.

Jess savored the trap that was about bout to be sprung on both men; especially Alec Campbell.

Chapter 24

Special Agent Anthony Cross's brow furrowed at the information that lay before him. He checked the sources for the information for a third time, but the outcome was the same. There was no doubt. There *was* an unsavory link between Alec Campbell and one of Metro City's finest, Sergeant Owen Meeks. Even after the evidence had been confirmed, he didn't want to accept it. The bureau and the justice department had spent months sweeping clean MCPD of its criminal element, but somehow this one had fallen between the cracks.

The information had been acquired from a private detective, Kobe West who worked for one of Metro City's prominent attorney's. He just happened to make a connection between the two while following up on another matter he was investigating.

He had just returned from a meeting with his superiors who informed him they had Rafe Santiago in custody on an unrelated matter; another one of the city's former police officers. What was it with this city's corrupt cops? They thought they had cleansed Metro City's police department after Wallace and his gang, but it seemed more had sprung up to take their place.

The information he held in his hands, was due to money in Meeks' bank account, all deposited in cash. The total over the last several months had equaled to two hundred thousand dollars, to which it seemed Meeks had no legitimate source to account for it. That kind of money had to be drawn from somewhere. What placed Meeks on the watch list were the amounts he deposited. Just like clockwork, Meeks stashed a little over nine thousand dollars per deposit in his personal account every three weeks. Anthony shook his head.

Somebody hadn't gotten the memo that the feds now flagged much lesser amounts than the previous ten grand limits; all due to 911 and the war on terror. Still he would not attribute the money above anything more than money laundering. Cops like Meeks usually accumulated their ill-gotten gains from the street hustlers; skimming a few dollars here and there after a big drug bust without drawing suspicion. But most had the good sense not to deposit the money in a bank. After his meeting, he had more than enough reason to follow the money.

This is where Campbell came in. No one in the bureau thought it was a coincidence that similar amounts were drawn from Campbell's accounts, nor did they have to speculate if the money was legit at this point. There was no good reason why a candidate for mayor would pay that amount of money to a lowly police sergeant that was not on the mayor-elect's campaign payroll. Granted, the money was taken from several of Campbell's accounts, but the totals always amounted to what Meeks deposited. Even though it looked incriminating, it was circumstantial at best. But what puzzled him the most was the money that was taken from his campaign account. That money was never accounted for.

"What the hell did he do with four hundred thousand?" The man could have just kept sloppy books, but Anthony didn't think so. A small portion from that account could have gone to Meeks, but what happened to the rest? This didn't look good either way he looked at it. Not having been briefed on the entire story involving Meeks or Campbell, he decided to pull the thread on what he did know and see where it lead him.

Agent Cross picked up the phone to contact Lt. Eric Valero. He would like for the detective to have an informal chat with Campbell to get his assessment on the matter, before the bureau got involved. He didn't want to taint the man if there was a legitimate reason for the withdrawals. But if money was paid to Meeks or someone else from campaign funds and weren't used for a campaign reasons, the bureau would jump in with both feet. After the Wallace debacle, Metro City's criminal indiscretions were pounced upon immediately.

After explaining his dilemma to the Lieutenant and gathering the assurance the matter would be handled, Agent Cross received a call from the Marshal's office. His eyes widened at what he was told. His case just became more complicated. Had he waited just a few seconds more, he would have had his answers. He prayed the call he just placed to MCPD didn't complicate things further for their case.

Chapter 25

Former Metro City District Attorney Jess Ashford stepped through the door just as Alec Campbell rose to his feet to leave Eric's office. Alec had had enough of all the speculation and innuendo. If they had something concrete on him, they would have been having this conversation in an interrogation room. But once he turned and saw Jess, he froze.

What is she doing here? Alec thought he was done with her months ago.

Every eye in the room was now focused on Jess who never took her eyes off of Alec. She stared at him with self-satisfied euphoria. She knew she was the last person he ever expected to see. He would have seen her before now, if she hadn't taken her task seriously enough to dot all I's and cross every necessary T. She wanted to make certain when she took this monster down, he had no wiggle room to skate free. This man's reign of terror was about to come to an end.

Once the FBI had compared their findings with those of hers during her talk with Rafe, she asked that she be the one to deliver the news to police headquarters, where Alec Campbell was currently being questioned. She envisioned the look on his face when she appeared and she was not disappointed.

As Jess moved further into the now over populated office, still eyeing Alec, her investigator Jimi Leigh Wilson stepped in behind her. No one seemed to notice the other woman, as all eyes were planted firmly on Jess. Jimi held her post by the door near Kobe, who raised a brow at this newcomer. She gave him a flirtatious wink and a smile before turning her attention to everyone else in the room as they eyed Jess. Each person beheld Jess as if she were an apparition.

Finally, just like Jess, Jimi especially focused on Alec Campbell; hoping he would make a run for it so she could knock him on his ass. She had been itching to put a beat down on him from the moment she uncovered his first transgression. She maybe female, but she was as tough as any man; maybe more so. Her host of brothers made sure she could hold her own. No one pushed their little sister around.

Indignant, Alec was the one to finally break the silence. "What the hell are you doing here?" So taken aback, he had forgotten he was supposed to be leaving and dropped back into the chair he just vacated.

"Aww, is that anyway to greet a former associate?" Jess asked him sarcastically.

Not have an appropriate retort, Alec's jaw clenched. As the situation stood, he thought it was best he continued to keep his mouth shut. His jaw was compressed so tight that a throbbing vein formed on his forehead, as he had a sinking feeling Jess's sudden appearance wasn't in his best interest. At this point, he hoped all they *could* prove was financial improprieties. But if Jess Ashford's superior stance was any indication that she knew a hell of a lot more, he was doomed.

Ignoring Alec for the moment, Landon rose from his seat on the corner of Eric's desk, where he had been lounging during the questioning. He too didn't think he would ever see Jess again.

"What *are* you doing here Jess?" The last time he saw her, she was flying off to parts unknown.

"I came to help you all out with your case or should I say *cases* against Alec here. In fact, I can clear up all the dead-end mysteries that have been plaguing this department for months." This certainly got everyone's attention, especially a stoic Alec.

She turned to Jimi. "This is my associate Jimi Wilson, who has quite a tale to tell *and* she has the documentation to back up every word." The occupants in the room barely gave Jimi a glance; still shocked Metro City's demonized former DA stood before them in the flesh.

Jess stood strong and tall in a pair of Gianvito Rossi pumps, that nicely complimented her perfectly tailored, navy skirt and trendy, but modest blouse. The jewelry she wore was simple, but as with her attire, expensive. Her stylish hair was longer; eyes and skin brighter. She looked good; better than good. She looked respectable! For a woman who slinked out of town under a cloud of shame, she stood before them fit, healthy and refreshed. Jess Ashford had always possessed an air about her that screamed confident and assured, but today, those traits were maximized. Wherever she landed and whatever she had been doing the past months had paid off in spades. Her entire demeanor said 'I'm back and with a vengeance'.

Upon hearing that indeed he was the purpose of her visit, Alec Campbell tried to remain unaffected by her superior stance. His outer appearance belied the internal turmoil that threatened to overtake him. If there was one thing he did recall about Jess Ashford, it was her thoroughness in her duties as prosecutor. So much so, it used to infuriate him. She was the best at her job and he knew it. That was the reason he had to get her out of Metro City.

Not missing Alec's presumable non-reaction, Jess returned her focus to the subject of her visit. "You see Alec made a mistake in thinking I would just fade away in the night and never return after he outed me to the world. For the length of time that I worked for him, he should have gotten to know me instead of wasting that time plotting against me. There was no way I was going to let whoever took my career away get away with it."

With this new revelation hitting the crowd, Jess turned her attention to Eric Valero, who had become uneasy with the sudden turn in the conversation. She read every emotion that slipped across his chiseled features.

At this, Eric slowly leaned forward in his chair and stared back as her. He didn't exactly know where Jess's story would take them, but he had a gut feeling by the end of it all, those eyes who were now studying Jess would soon be turning in his direction and not with any admiration. This little chat they were having may very well turn into what could be trouble for him.

Jess let her gaze linger a few seconds more on the lieutenant, before addressing the group in general. "From the looks on your faces, I can see you had no idea it was your precious mayor elect here who tried to destroy me."

When her statement collided with stunned silence, she continued. "I worked as an associate prosecutor under Alec in Elgin, before taking the position here in Metro City. He was one of the reasons I accepted the job. When we worked together, he couldn't stand that I out shined him and would look for ways to undermine me every chance he got. I knew I had to leave before he started digging around in my personal life and revealed my secrets. Little did I know, he knew them all. I probably would have been better off staying put, because landing the job as head prosecutor posed a bigger problem for him. And had I known his ambition was to become mayor here, I probably would have stayed in Elgin." She shrugged with the uncertainty of it all.

She continued to stare at Alec, who couldn't meet her gaze. He had doubled down on ignoring her. She felt if he ground his teeth any harder, his jaw would shatter before their eyes.

"I'm sure you all recall how that nasty business with the priest, who was caught up with Craven fell apart without him being jailed right along with his cohorts." She gestured with her chin. "This is the man who helped him skirt the law and in return, the good father gifted him every video and photo he had accumulated of me and my friends." Jess now had everyone's attention, a part from her mere presence. All eyes landed on Alec and they all saw him with a new vision.

"Alec's attack on me was twofold. First, he hated me because I was a better prosecutor and probably rejoiced when I resigned—until he learned where I was headed. When I landed the DA position, he needed me out of Metro City, because he knew he couldn't control me. If I had been allowed to stay after he won the election, he *had* to work with me. And that would spell trouble for him, because I was in a position of not having to take his shit without questions. But with me gone, he could do whatever he pleased."

Eric came out of his stupor and spoke up. Asking the question he was sure everyone one present wanted to know. "Why was it so important that you not be district attorney?"

Jess smiled. They had so much to learn about their new mayor. "Alec is one of the original members of Craven Wallace's band of merry criminals. A member that only Craven knew existed. And I say *is*, because their enterprising ventures never ceased. Some of the players may have changed, but the game didn't. The whole purpose of Alec claiming the mayoral office was to be in the perfect position to help Craven grow his operation from behind bars, netting them all an even greater gain in profits."

The shock around the room was so thick it was palpable. They had no idea. Each of the occupants turned one to the other; trying to come to grips as to how they all missed it.

"Have any of you checked on your notorious former mayor lately?" Jess continued. "I'll take your silence as a no. Well, you would find that he and the former police chief live like kings in prison. And with Alec at the helm, funneling any needed resources their way, they would be unstoppable. Who knows? With his underhanded skills at manipulating the system and freeing criminals, the group could very easily be released and walking free among us without us becoming the wiser."

Jess glanced around the room. Everyone present was floored. Here they were having a sit down over possible misappropriation of campaign funds, when there was more on Alec than any of them could have ever known.

"Now that you have a taste of what this man is capable of, I'll let Jimi give you the 'more' portion of this little meeting." While the room was still reeling, Jess stepped aside and motioned for Jimi to continue with the rest.

Jimi dramatically cleared her throat for emphasis before sashaying to the front of the room, where she sat a bulging messenger bag on Eric's desk with a thud. She winked at Landon who had finally taken notice of her and was staring at her open-mouthed.

Today Jimi was dressed in the tightest dark blue jeans he had ever seen a woman wear, paired with a hot pink cropped top that barely contained her generous breasts. Over the skimpy top, she wore a sleeveless navy blue, button down shirt that stopped short of covering her generous behind. Jimi's feet were clad in impossibly tall heels in the same shade of pink as her top and well-manicured nails. The color that covered her full lips was a shade or two darker, but pink nevertheless. Her long lush eyelashes framed eyes that seemed to sparkle mischievously in the dim light.

Pleased that it was now her turn to shine, Jimi gathered a hand full of blond, waist length, box braids and maneuvered them over her left shoulder before turning to Landon. The move placed emphasis on a narrow track of tattooed animal prints that marched from behind Jimi's earlobe, twisting around the back of her neck, where Landon assumed ended somewhere across her back. The tiny, delicate prints were pink, outlined in black. He rationalized her favorite color *had* to be pink.

"Landon Payne, I guess I will start with you."

At his surprised reaction to her speaking to him as if she knew him, Jimi winked at Landon again. *He* certainly didn't know *her*. He'd never seen the woman before in his life. And there was no way he would have missed a character such as Jimi Leigh Wilson. He made a mental note to get up to speed on this woman once this meeting was over.

"Your good friend and former coworker Rafe Santiago was the person who shot you…and this brings me to you Detective…um forgive me, Lieutenant Valero." Jimi swung her head around, repositioning her blond tresses with the move. With her attitude and sing-song cadence of her voice, she didn't give any of them time to react to the news, before she plowed forward.

"Oh, before I forget." Jimi reached into her tight back pocket; producing Landon's pen, which she handed over with a flourish. "I'll explain that later," she grinned at him when he noticed the plump behind that the pen had been resting against.

Landon lifted his eyes to stare at her. He thought he had lost the pen, never dreaming someone had taken it. Never dreaming *she* had taken it.

"Now back to you," she told Eric; pointing at him with one of those bubble gum pink nails. "Santiago also shot your wife." Once this bomb was dropped, the outrage grew to the level of deafening.

Completely caught off guard, Eric almost knocked over his chair when he sprang from it.

"What? Rafe …Why? And what does any of this have to do with him." This was from Landon, who pointed at Alec. As for Eric, his mind was racing all over the place. He just stood there; too blown away to form the words for the questions he had.

Alec sat as if he were made of stone; neither reacting nor speaking. The only indication that he was aware of what Jimi said, was the minute gesture of closing his eyes against his coming sins involving Santiago. Alec knew the moment Jimi mentioned Rafe's name he knew it was over for him.

"I will tell you, if you will let me continue," Jimi rolled her eyes at Landon's interruption. "Although Lieutenant, this involves you even more than anyone else in this sad saga."

Jimi's eyes regrettably landed on Eric's ashen face. Yes, this next part of the story may very well cost him his job. She hoped not. From what she could tell, he was a decent person and didn't deserve to go down with the likes of Alec Campbell. If she could have omitted him from this, she would have; but there had been too many secrets; secrets that cost lives.

Believing he knew what was coming, Eric fell back into his chair with a plop. He had so many questions. Even Landon had returned to his seat on the corner of Eric's desk. Kobe, speechless, retained his stance in the corner; waiting for the rest of the story. Jess had found a vacant chair near the door. She folded her arms while Jimi spoke. She was too full of rage at what all Alec had involved himself in to comment. That was why she allowed Jimi to lay it all out for them. Not only had this piece of shit hurt her, but he had ruined so many other lives in the wake of his self-aggrandizing storm.

"My employer, Jess…" Jimi glanced at her. "Was the reason that you both were targeted." Jimi let that sink in before she continued. "After Alec sent his life destroying package to the lieutenant, Rafe found out that Landon had been with Jess too, although the evidence of his involvement wasn't among the others who were exposed. As you all know, Rafe Santiago was fired. The thing is, Rafe hadn't know about Landon until Alec told him. Alec was so pleased with the way you handled it all Lieutenant, he shot his mouth off without foreseeing the future consequences."

Jimi paused here. The next part would fully implicate Eric, but there was nothing else she could do but continue.

"Campbell informed Rafe that you were the one who leaked the package to the press and that you were the one who kept Landon's name out of it, along with his brother's."

Kobe thought he would develop whiplash from his head swiveling from Landon to Eric and back again. He had no clue the Payne brothers were involved with Jess, let alone Eric's part in the exposure. This was like the Wallace case all over again. They thought they were investigating one thing and found it was only the tip of the iceberg. Kobe began to feel as if he had been punched.

Unconcerned with the room's dizzying astonishment, Jimi continued. "Rafe hated you Landon because you got off scot free while he lost everything; his job, his family, everything. And you Eric, (Jimi dropped the title, considering she knew all of his intimate secrets), he blamed you for it all. He couldn't understand how you could protect Landon and not him too."

"Oh my god…what have I done?" Eric was horrified. Had he known for one instant that the backlash for his decision would have nearly cost Landon and his wife's lives, he would never have leaked the damning information.

Jimi felt sorry for him, but it was her job. She gave Eric a moment before she continued. "So Landon, to get even, he set you up to be shot. He meant to kill you but you were lucky that day. And Eric, he planned to kill you too, until he read of your wedding announcement. He thought killing your wife would be fair, since you caused him to lose his."

Eric quickly cycled from horrified at the results of his actions, to rage. Rafe Santiago almost killed KT because he felt slighted. "All that asshole had to do was keep it in his pants. He was married for god's sake! The Payne brothers were single and would—"

He cut the sentence off after realizing his mistake. Jon and Landon *were* single and would have weathered the storm just fine. Landon would probably have made detective in spite of it all. He was wrong and it took the near death of his wife and colleague for him to come to terms with that fact.

Kobe finally spoke up. "How do you know all of this? Where is Santiago now?"

Jess took this. "Rafe Santiago is across town in federal lock up. We thought it was best considering those who tell tales against this man seem to end up dead," Jess told them; indicating Alec who groaned with this new information. He was hoping Santiago was dead and at the very least had left the country.

Eric vacated his chair again; this time to confront Rafe. He couldn't sit there any longer. He knew he had to answer for what he had done with the videos and photos, but right now he had to look the man in the eye who tried his best to kill his wife. He would worry about disciplinary actions later. But if truth were to be told, he didn't care if they fired him. He was just grateful KT survived the maniac's rampage.

No one bothered to stop him as he tore out of his office nearly taking the door off its hinges. They all knew where he was headed and why.

After Eric left, Landon had a question. "I can understand why Rafe wanted to hurt Eric; I even understand why he wanted me dead. But the information I received about the connection to the Kane murder…"

Kobe finished for him. "Was that just a rouse to get Landon out to ambush him or—"

"Or Rafe was the one who killed Alonso Kane?" Jimi finished with a raised brow. She nodded in the affirmative. "Yes, he was the one who executed Alonso Kane."

"But why?!" Landon shouted. This time leaving the desk for good. He needed to pace; to try and get some sort of understanding. Every time he thought he had a grasp on the events of this mess, there was another twist or turn in the narrative. "How is Rafe and Kane connected?"

"Because of this piece of shit." Jess had vacated her spot at the door and had taken Eric's chair. She wanted to look the murdering monster in his eyes when Jimi continued.

All eyes were once again on Alec Campbell, who, out of anger, was shaking like a drug deprived addict. He knew it was over for him and there was nothing that he could do to stop it. He just wished he could have gotten his hands on Santiago. The man was his undoing.

"You have to understand. Rafe Santiago was working for Alec long before he went after you and Eric. Rafe was his henchman; his go to guy for all things unsavory that needed to be accomplished for him to become mayor," Jimi informed them.

For Landon, some parts of this saga from hell was coming together. They were so caught up in Rafe targeting him and Eric no one had bothered to ask the obvious question. What was Alec's link to Rafe? But even with that question answered, there was another that begged to be asked. What did Alonso Kane have to do with any of this?

As if reading his mind, Jimi continued. "Alonso Kane was Alec's long lost son," Jimi told them.

"Wait a damn minute; what?" Landon halted his pacing immediately. This was beyond incredible!

Jess nodded. "Yep, Alonso Kane and Shelby Kirkland's *loving* dad," she added sweetly, while Campbell finally conceded and dropped his head. They knew everything.

"My God," Kobe moaned.

Having had enough of looking at Alec Campbell's pathetic face, Jess moved to open the door to a pair of officers waiting just outside to cart Alec off to a holding cell, before being transported to the county jail. She pointed to Alec who was catatonic upon hearing his crimes displayed before him. Even he was grateful to be dismissed from whatever else Jimi and Jess had to reveal.

After Alec was led away, Jimi addressed Landon. She knew he had questions that should have been simple to answer, but had become complicated due to Alec's diabolical ministrations.

"Landon, I understand you were looking into the whereabouts of the sibling's parents." Landon nodded; still trying to wrap his mind around all that had been revealed that day with more still to come.

"Well, the reason you couldn't find them at least their father, was because Alec changed his name and erased his former life. The name he goes under now belongs to a deceased young man whose life he assumed after the real Alec Campbell's parents died. He assumed his name after he went away to college. With all the people who could have exposed him as a fraud dead, he could be whomever he wanted; everyone except his son that is. Kane knew exactly who he was and would have exposed him the moment he threw his hat in the ring for mayor under the alias."

"What about his daughter, Shelby?" Kobe asked. He too was trying to make sense of it all.

"Shelby was assumed safe, because she was an infant when he abandoned them. And since there were no known photos of either of their parents, she couldn't identify him," Jimi explained.

"And just in case you're wondering. I have all of the proof right here, along with Santiago's statement." Jimi patted the messenger bag.

Landon spoke again. "He had his mother's home burned down after Kane was killed." It was more of a statement than a question. Landon was seeing everything clearly now. The man was tying up every loose end.

"All of this because he wanted to be mayor?" Kobe's mind couldn't handle anymore. Could money and power mean that much to this man that he killed his own child?

"I hope like hell this is the last of Craven Wallace's dynasty. I don't think I can handle any more of this." Deciding to leave, Kobe gave the remaining group members one last glance before stepping through the door. He'd had enough for the day.

Landon released a long slow sigh. He needed a drink. Hell he needed a few drinks.

Chapter 26

"We interrupt this program to bring you breaking news," news anchor Jocelyn Sanders was informing her viewing audience.

"Metro City's mayor elect, Alec Campbell has been arrested on murder charges. The newly elected mayor, who has yet to be sworn into office, was asked to a meeting at Metro City Police Headquarters this morning, concerning misappropriation of campaign funds. We are told, before he could be connected with the crime, formerly disgraced DA, Jess Ashford, crashed the meeting with viable information that led to his arrest. We have field reporter Ted Callahan standing by to give us more information, Ted."

"That's right Jocelyn. My sources tell me Jess Ashford did indeed drop a major bomb in that meeting today. From what I could gather, Alec Campbell had his son, the notorious gangbanger, Alonso Kane, murdered to secure his bid for mayor. Although no one is talking as to why Kane's death was important, we hope to get further details as this newest scandal unfolds."

"Ted, we are getting reports that police officer and former bodyguard to Ashford, Rafe Santiago, is involved. Is this true?" Jocelyn asked.

"Yes Jocelyn. I've learned that Rafe Santiago, one of the former DA's outed sexual partners, was hired by Campbell to murder Alonso Kane. As you may recall, Santiago was fired from Metro City PD because of his inappropriate conduct with the former D.A. It is rumored

Santiago is also responsible for shooting police Lieutenant Eric Valero's wife, Kaitlin Valero at their wedding. And from what I understand, there are more charges pending in both of the men's cases. Back to you Jocelyn."

Ryan and Virginia set in his media room stunned at the news. Neither of them could utter a word. They had just come in from dinner and were enjoying a glass of wine when the news interrupted the television show they were barely watching. Instead, they were enjoying their time together when they heard Alec Campbell's name mentioned.

Alec Campbell arrested for murder with other charges pending. How could this have happened?

Ryan opened his mouth to ask that very question when his phone rang. Not knowing what else to do, he answered it. Virginia sat in stunned horror while Ryan took the call.

"Yes this is Ryan Hamilton." Ryan listened for a few moments before telling the caller, "No comment," and ending the call. There were several more calls before he turned his mobile phone off. He needed to digest this new information without interruption.

Finally turning her attention away from the television, Virginia focused on Ryan. "What's wrong?"

Ryan placed his face in his palms, trying to understand it all. "The calls were from reporters asking if the rumors were true."

"What rumors?"

"It seems, since Campbell has been arrested, he has forfeited his right to become mayor, especially since he hasn't been sworn in. And according to them, I'm now Metro City's mayor."

"What? Oh my God, Ryan! That's wonderful!" Virginia was bouncing in her seat. "Do you think it's true?"

Ryan shook his head. "I guess we'll find out soon enough." Deciding that he needed more information he turned his phone back on to make a call, only to have it ring the moment it connected. This time the call was from election officials summoning him for a meeting. He would find out within the hour what his chances were of becoming Metro City's new mayor.

∞

Ryan and Virginia sat holding hands in the election commissioner's office listening to the policies and regulations that were being read to them. At the end of the citation, they both were stunned a second time that day. After all of the campaigning and then losing the election, Ryan Hamilton was now Metro City's newly appointed mayor.

After Alec was charged, anyone remotely connected to him wanted no parts of the office. So since Ryan had the most votes second to Alec, he was declared the victor.

"All of this does hinge on a more thorough investigation by just about every federal agency of course," the commissioner was saying. Under the circumstances, I'm sure you understand we have to do a second background check on your..." the commissioner cleared his throat...character. But I don't foresee any reasons why you will not be our new mayor, unless you have skeletons in your closet that would prevent it."

Although the man was joking, he hoped like hell Ryan didn't. Metro City had had its fill of scandal and was in need of a leader it could trust. They didn't need any more surprises and hoped Alec Campbell was the last of the bedlam for a very long time to come.

Ryan beamed. "I can assure you Commissioner. I have nothing to hide and will bring nothing but honor to the office and this great city."

"Good to hear. Now if you will just look over these papers and attach your signature then we can get the ball rolling Mr. Mayor."

The commissioner grinned. He felt good about having Ryan Hamilton as mayor. He never approved of Alec Campbell. Something with the man was off. He was overjoyed his choice would now hold the city's highest office.

Ryan squeezed Virginia's hand.

Chapter 27

"Hey Sy, how is she?" Matthias asked.

Syon was reclined in a chair near Queen's bed watching a baseball game on the wall mounted television. He was still sore but had healed enough to be released from medical care. But he wasn't about to leave until Queen left to go home with him.

He smiled. "Good news. The small amount of swelling she had has gone down and her brain is back to normal. Jon expects for her to wake up anytime now."

Matthias let out a sigh of relief. The news was good to hear. "Here, I brought you some food. And I want you to eat it. It won't do Queen any good if you go down." He handed his brother a hefty cardboard takeout box.

Syon opened the container to inhale the delicious aroma. His stomach growled. He couldn't remember the last time he actually ate a full meal. Whenever he left the hospital, it was to shower and change clothes, but not for food. He had been too worried to eat. But now that Queen was returning to good health, he was ravenous. Taking the huge triple cheeseburger, with grilled onions, mayo and tomato from its wrapper, he took a bite and closed his eyes; savoring the perfectly seasoned gourmet burger's succulent flavor.

"The food is compliments of Landon Payne," Matthias informed him.

Syon nodded before shoving some equally delicious fries into his still full mouth. Landon sent food from *Randy's* to the hospital for them and the officers who were guarding Queen, every day she was there. He felt it was the least he could do. He and Queen were still friends.

Matthias looked over at Queen. "She's better too."

Syon nodded again. "Jon says she's healing nicely. I am so grateful. It could have been a lot worse. I could have lost them both. According to the gynecologist, she can still have children," he told his brother around a mouth full of food. He took the strawberry shake Matthias handed him to wash it all down.

Syon was grateful Queen was spared, but he still mourned the loss of their child. He dreaded having to share that bitter news once she woke up. He took another bite of his burger; needing to chew away the pain that threatened to return.

"I stopped by the precinct before I came here. I wanted to know if there was any news on your case. I caught Kobe on the way out and man, he's messed up." Matthias swiped a hand over his closely cropped hair.

Syon wiped his mouth with a paper napkin. "What's going on?"

"Our newly elected mayor was just book on murder charges among other things."

Syon nearly choked on the fries he just popped into his mouth. "What the hell are you talking about? Murder? Who did he murder?

"According to Kobe, he had his son killed. And you'll never guess who his son was... Alonso Kane."

"The murdered gangbanger was his son?" Syon abandoned his food altogether, while his brother relayed everything that had happen at police headquarters that day.

"Can this town get a mayor that isn't crooked?" Syon shook his head.

Matthias nodded. "Since the news hit that Campbell had been arrested, anyone who was remotely connected to him are scattering in all directions. So it looks like Ryan Hamilton will be our mayor. And believe me; the feds will go over his life with a fine tooth comb to make sure we don't get any more ugly surprises.

"You know; Campbell always felt shady to me after his creepy interest in Queen. But after that, I hadn't given him much thought. But never in my wildest dreams would I have thought he was that terrible."

"Hey! Who's eating a *Randy's* burger and not offering me any?"

Syon and Matthias both froze and turned towards the bed. Queen was groggy but awake.

"Oh my God! Baby, you're awake!" Placing the box of food on the bedside stand, Syon came to his feet to take her into his arms; being careful of her broken arm. "Oh, baby I was so worried."

"What happened? How did I get here?" Queen was confused by her surroundings.

Matthias backed out of the room to give them some privacy. What Syon had to tell her would be tough and they didn't need an audience.

Chapter 28

Kobe drove straight to Blake's after leaving the police station. He couldn't believe what Alec had done in order to become mayor. He killed his own son. What kind of monster would do that to his child?

Kobe left the meeting—or the unveiling of Alec Campbell's crimes—feeling as if a ton of bricks had landed on him. How the hell had he missed all of that? He fancied himself an above average investigator and found it hard to believe that he hadn't been the one who uncovered all that was Alec Campbell. Not only had he not been the one to bring the murdering son of a bitch down, but a woman. He would not have guessed in a hundred years Jimi Leigh Wilson was a private investigator let along a top one. He had to hand it to Jimi; the ostentatious woman was on top of her game. And after what he just witnessed, he would definitely have to step up his.

He shook his head. In reality he knew he couldn't blame himself. He, like everyone else in Eric's office, never even considered Alec more than a swindler at best. The small thread he came across was so minute, he nearly missed it. Something was nagging him about something Syon had said about Campbell that placed him on his trail in the first place. Although bothered, he didn't expect to find anything. So when he stumbled upon the payoffs to people who had nothing to do with his campaign, he thought the man was just using the funds for personal use, not to commit unspeakable crimes.

But for him, the day's biggest shocker had been
Eric. Of the time he knew Eric Valero, he had been nothing
short of a man with the most integrity. Although he tore out
of the office before he could explain his reasoning for
creating the Jess Ashford scandal, Kobe wanted to believe
everything he did was for a sane purpose; from Jess's
exposure, to the protection of the Payne brothers. He hoped
for KT's sake he wasn't involved in anything nefarious.
But at this point, everyone was suspect.

Kobe swiped a hand down his face as he stood on
Blake's doorstep waiting for her to answer the bell. He
needed to bury himself in her loving arms to feel some sort
of normalcy after hearing the crimes of Alec Campbell. He
wouldn't even allow himself to dwell on what Eric had
done. He would have to meditate on that later. But right
now, he just needed his love's comfort.

When Blake opened the door, he immediately knew
something was wrong. Her anxious expression said it all.
He didn't have to wait long to discover what was the source
of her distress. He immediately heard Janice Steele's voice
reverberating from within. Janice was demanding Blake tell
whoever was at the door to go away, because they had
more important things to discuss. Kobe had been so caught
up in the day's events, he had failed to notice Janice's car
parked in the circular driveway.

Before he could stop himself, without a word, Kobe
pushed past Blake and stalked into the room where Janice
was holding court. Today was not the day he could hold his
tongue with the infuriating woman, not after the day he just

had. All the frustration and rage that he felt came bubbling to the top to over flow in the direction of Blake's mother. He'd had enough of Janice Steele.

"You hateful, selfish, ungrateful bitch! All the things that your daughter has done for you and you are still unappreciative? You are the reason your son is sitting in prison now. With a mother like you, Derrick didn't have a chance. But do you know what? Your daughter will have more than a chance to be loved the way she should have been by someone who calls herself a mother. I love her and will make sure she knows that each and every day. I will spend the rest of my life erasing every evil, hateful thing you have done or said to her! And lady, if you ever speak anything other than graciousness toward this awesome woman, I will make you sorrier than you have ever been in your life! Now get the hell out of here before I do something we both will regret!" Kobe pointed towards the door for emphasis.

You would have thought someone had set Janice on fire the way she grabbed up her purse and ran from Blake's home.

Blake stood in the middle of the floor with her hands covering her mouth, watching Kobe rein in his emotions. She was so moved, tears streamed from her eyes. She had never seen him like that before. No one, not even her father had taken up for her like that. Kobe had his back to her. His chest was still heaving from the outburst. When he turned, he saw her tears.

He stepped to her, pulling her into his arms. "Baby, I am sorry but I couldn't stand to hear one more negative word towards you from that woman."

Blake shook her head before pulling back enough to look up at him. "You have nothing to apologize for. Kobe, that was amazing! I loved you before you stuck up for me, but now, I love you even more!" She kissed him then. He loved her. That in its self, made Janice's behavior worth enduring.

Kobe lifted her into his arms. He was about to show her just how much he loved her.

Chapter 29

Commander Nedra Scott sat in her office gazing at Eric Valero who could not meet her eyes. He messed up and knew he was in trouble. Once the news broke that Alec had been arrested, he had been the top story of the day. But they both knew as soon as the media had beat that horse to death they would come for him.

Resigned, Nedra sighed. "Even though Alec Campbell is the main actor in this drama, your actions set off a whole other string of events. Your leaking that…that package, for lack of a better word, resulted in people being shot and could have been killed. It was a true blessing neither Payne nor your wife weren't killed."

Eric sat silently while his boss talked; covering ground that he had already dragged himself over. If he had guessed for one second the horrible repercussions his actions would have caused, he would never have sent the package to *Do Tail*.

"Do you want to tell me why you sent that trash to that gossip rag?" She thought she knew why, wanted to hear it from him. At this point, the police commissioner, her boss, left it in her hands as to how to discipline him.

Eric sat up straight and cleared his throat. "It was a matter of time before Alec would have publicized the whole mess. And no, I didn't know he was the one behind it all until Jess informed us. Anyway, I thought if I could get ahead of it all, it would stop or at least take the air of the culprit's sails. Alec was hell bent on destroying Jess one way or another. I just threw a wrench in the works to minimize the impact—or so I thought." Eric shrugged. In hindsight, he made a bigger mess.

Nedra nodded. "I thought as much. I just wish you would have informed me of your plans and maybe we could have avoided some of these mishaps…or maybe not; we will never know." She folded her hands under her chin before she spoke again.

"Your discipline was left up to me by the commissioner, whom I assume wants no parts of this. He didn't out and out say it, but I think he may have done the same thing had he been in that position. Who knows, I may have done something similar. Anyway, I'm recommending that you take two weeks leave without pay. I am not punishing you for leaking the files, but for you not keeping me in the loop. Like you said, the garbage was bound to be dumped had you done nothing. And, I am going to give you another two weeks without pay, because you removed the Payne brothers from the files. If you were going to leak them, you should have leaked them all and let the chips fall where they may."

"Oh, and you might want to avoid Jack Hanolin for a while. He wants to know why you didn't protect him. But I suspect he is all bark and no bite; the scandal didn't touch him since he too is a single man. Although…his ex-wife might want to know if he slept with Jess before or after their divorce. At anything rate, he got a lot of 'atta boys' from his male counterparts, so he's just fine."

It was Nedra's turn to shrug. It was just like men to praise a man for sleeping around, but if a woman does it, she is instantly condemned.

"Who will handle the division while I'm out?" He hoped it would be in capable hands. He didn't need to come back to a mess."

"Oh yeah that. Jack will take the reins while you're out. It was only fair since…"

"I get it." Eric rose to leave. "Thank you Nedra, for everything." Nedra nodded. She knew he was including the support she gave him and KT.

Eric let out a huge sigh of relief once he left Nedra's office. He hadn't know what to expect when he was summoned for the meeting. He didn't mind the month off, he was grateful he still had his job and rank. Either could have been pulled. Having an idea, he called his travel agent. Even though KT was still on the mend, she didn't have to do it in Metro City as long as she took it easy. It was time they took their honeymoon.

Chapter 30

Queen sat propped up in her bed watching the local news. It had been a few days since she felt like doing anything other than cry. After Syon explained what happened and that they lost their child, she had retreated into herself. Someone had taken their baby away. Everyone tried to cheer her up. Once Cymone and Myka discovered she was conscious, they came to her aid. They all cried together. They hadn't known about the baby either. She wanted Syon to be the first to know. After Cymone and Myka left, Landon stopped by, bringing a *Randy's* burger of her own. But even he couldn't draw her out of her despair.

She and Syon had a deep ache that would always be there, but she wished she knew why it happened. Who hated her enough to want her dead? She didn't have any enemies. Landon told her of their suspicions that the first incident was indeed an attempt on her life. She had racked her brain trying to understand why this was happening to her. She couldn't come up with anyone other than Allison and she was still locked up. There was no one else who would harm her.

She was about to change the channel when Alec Campbell's photo came on the screen. The newscaster was relaying the story for the hundredth time. But when they place the photos of Shelby and Kane next to Alec, something clicked into place for Queen. She stared hard at the trio, trying to focus on what was so important about them.

Then she knew. Memories of her childhood came flooding back. She remembered! "OH MY GOD!!!

Syon was just returning with dinner for them when she shouted. He quickly placed the food on a table after witnessing her agitated state.

"Sy, Sy I remember!" Queen was nearly coming off the bed. If it hadn't been for the cast on her leg she would have leaped from it. "Oh my God, I remember!"

"Baby what's wrong? You remember what?"

Queen pointed at the television. "Alec or whatever his name is…I remember! I know where I've seen Alec Campbell before."

"Baby calm down." Syon wanted her to calm down before she injured her healing body. He gently pressed her back against the mound of pillows.

"Okay, Where?" Syon's eyes narrowed. From the look of shock on Queen's face, he didn't think he was going to like her answer.

"At our house! The house me and mama shared before she died. But he's not how I remember him though, not exactly. I know people change as they grow older, but it's his voice that I remember the most. The man I remember was much heavier and had a beard. But still there is something different about his face without the beard.

Nope, he didn't like this one bit.

"I was young, in maybe first or second grade, so it's no wonder I forgot. Mama and I were sitting in the living room going over my homework that day, when someone knocked on the door. Mama got up to peek through the blinds to see who was there. I remember her eyes widening and her putting her finger to her lips for me to be quiet, before whispering to me to take all of my things and go into my room and close the door. She told me to be very quiet and not make a sound and she would come and get me when it was safe. I didn't understand what she was talking about but I did as she said." Queen's voice had become steady; her gaze staring off into the past.

"Only a few minutes had passed, but in my child's mind, she was taking too long to come, so I snuck out to take a peek at what was going on. From my vantage point, I could see the entire room and everyone in it through the huge mirror on the opposite wall. So I didn't have to be in the room to see the room. The first thing I noticed was that all of the pictures of me were gone. I found out later mama had hidden them in a drawer."

"The next thing I noticed was the man who was sitting on the couch with mama. I had never seen him before. They were arguing, so I stayed really quiet and still in my hiding place. I don't know what they were arguing about, but when the man left, mama was angry. The man was Alec Campbell, I'm certain of it. But that wasn't what she called him. Mama called him David or Davis; something like that."

"Did he see you?" Syon's eyes were mere slits by now. His mind was working a mile a minute. Knowing what he already knew about Alec Campbell, he wondered if he had anything to do with their crash.

Queen shook her head. "No, there was no way he could see me from where I was hiding, but I think mama knew I was there, even though she couldn't see me when she looked up into the mirror. I was standing in the shadows."

"Later, after he left, I asked her who was he. She just said he was someone she knew a long time ago and left it at that. She never brought him up again and I never saw him again, until that night at your sister's dinner party.

Syon slowly turned over what she just told him. *If he didn't see her, why did he look as if he*—? "Do you have a photo of your mother?" Things were starting to come together in his mind.

Queen nodded "Get my phone from the drawer.

Syon handed her the phone. "I scanned this one of her and emailed it to myself so she would always be with me. This is the last one she took before she died. Sometimes when I miss her so much, I just look at her photo and it brings me comfort."

Syon took one look at a smartly dressed Maureen Willis and understood Campbell's shock. Queen was the spitting image of her mother. They had the same build, the same eyes; the same smooth skin. Although she did resemble Maureen more, Queen had other features that did not match her mother's. He tapped the screen before handing the phone back to her.

"She's why Campbell was spooked. When he saw you, he saw your mother, probably about your age at the time. He must have thought he had stepped back in the past." He had another thought. "Could he be your father?" he asked quietly.

Queen shrugged. "Who knows? Whenever I brought up any questions of my father, mama would change the subject. But it would explain why she hid the photos, but why? Why would she not tell me? And from his reaction, I can guess that he never knew I existed."

But there was another question that plagued Syon. If Alec did guess that Queen was his daughter why hadn't he contacted her, even if it was just to prove that she wasn't? That gut feeling he had just turned up a notch. If Campbell had his son murdered, what would stop him from doing the same to Queen?

Syon turned his attention from Alec Campbell to take a long scrutinizing look at Queen. Taking her phone again, he pulled up a photo of Alec Campbell on the phone's web browser and looked at her again. He could clearly see Maureen in her, but was Alec there too? Try as he might, there was no resemblance that he could see. But she did say his appearance had changed somehow. Could he be her father? He didn't know, but he would get to the bottom of the mystery as soon as she was asleep for the night.

Before he put the phone on the night stand, he scrolled through the man's biography. Alec Campbell's middle name was Jackson, not David or Davis; just in case Maureen called him by his middle name. If the two were one and the same, why had he changed his name or was Davis or David the alias? Was he Alonso and Shelby's illegitimate father or was he married. The more he dug into the man, the more questions he had.

Turning his attention back to Queen again, he would let it rest for now. But the moment he could leave, he was headed directly to the police station. He was going to get to the bottom of this. And if Campbell was responsible for the loss of their child, God help him!

Chapter 31

Alec sat in an interrogation room wondering what they wanted to pin on him now. Eric Valero had already had a few choice words for him about letting Santiago loose on his wife. He tried to explain that he had nothing to do with that. How could he predict Santiago would go off the rails like that? Even though he didn't shoot either Valero's wife or Detective Payne, he was being held fully responsible. It was just another charge added to his already over worked account.

While he sat pondering his fate, he visibly stiffened when the door opened and Agent Anthony Cross stepped inside joined by Syon Bennett. Cross had been put in charge of his case and had kept the fires stoked with charge after charge. Alec didn't have to wonder why Syon was there. He figured they solve the mystery of the car accidents. It didn't matter. He was going to be spending the rest of his life in prison anyway, so he had nothing to lose.

Syon eyed him. He wanted very much to strangle the man sitting across from him. But looking at Alec, a small pathetic version of the man he first met at his sister's gathering, he knew he would get his just due spending many years behind bars. The man should thank his lucky stars their state didn't have the death penalty for what he'd done. But if Syon or law enforcement thought they knew all there was to know about Alec Campbell, aka Davis Kane, they were about to be in for a shock.

Agent Cross, known to his colleagues as AC, addressed Alec. "Campbell, Mr. Bennett here would like to ask you a few questions to which I too am curious to know the answers."

Although AC reluctantly granted Syon's request to see the prisoner, he needed answers. And if what Syon had speculated, concerning Alec Campbell were true, he would be adding more charges to his already long list after the meeting was over. But in order for the meeting to take place, he implored Syon to stay seated and keep his hands to himself, no matter what Campbell had to say. The first sign of trouble, the agents standing just beyond the closed door, were ready to spring into action. He didn't want to have to lock Syon up as well. Syon was a friend and he wanted to keep him out of trouble.

Alec pressed his shackled hands between his knees while he considered Syon. He knew the big man would be trouble for him from the first time he met him. He should have left Queen alone, but he didn't know what she knew about him. He didn't know what Maureen had told her. He didn't need for her to call him out after he became mayor to mess up his plans, but now all that was a moot point.

"What is it you want to know," he finally asked the expectant man.

"Is Queen your daughter?"

Bingo! She did know. Now if his plans of eliminating her had come to fruition he wouldn't be facing him right now. But then again; at this point why should it matter.

Alec nodded. "I knew the moment I laid eyes on her. Besides the fact she looks just like her mother, I can see some of my mother in her. She looks like me before…" he trailed off. That was another subject he would have to explain.

"Before what?" This was from AC.

He drew in a deep sigh and released it before he answered. "Before I had a little work done," he informed them; pointing to his face. "You know. A little nip here; a tuck there. Not much; just enough." Alec shrugged.

Syon and AC looked at one another. They didn't see that one coming. But for Syon, it explained Queen's statement that Alec really didn't resemble the person she remembered as a child. He just assumed it was because of her age that she may not have remembered what he looked like. Now he knew differently.

Syon spread his hands out across the table top before him. "Why did you have cosmetic surgery?" Even as he asked the question dread settled in his stomach like a lead weight. Something told him the answer maybe more than he or AC could handle. It was that glint that suddenly appeared in his eyes. It was sinister; it was so unnerving that it sent a shiver down his spine. He had a feeling they were about to meet Davis Kane.

AC sat up straight. He too felt they were in for a surprise. He made a gesture to his colleagues who was observing on the other side of the mirrored wall to start recording. Once he was certain the camera was rolling, he turned his attention back to Alec who was grinning.

"I changed my appearance to distance myself from my family—my mother and children. I did it to hide in plain sight."

"Kane and Shelby?" AC asked.

Alec nodded. "Kane was the only one living who could recognize me, even with the change."

"What do you mean by 'living'? AC had taken over the questioning. Syon sat with his own thoughts. How was he going to inform Queen that she was indeed the daughter of a killer?

Alec shrugged. "After I killed Alonso and Shelby's mother, my son was the only person who could recognize me," Alec simple informed him. "No matter what I did to my face, I couldn't really change my voice or mannerisms. And like I said I only had a little work done. My handsome face was probably the only decent thing my parents ever gave me, so I didn't want to alter it too much." Still grinning Alec shrugged again.

"Before my mother Elsa passed, god rest her soul, she told me Kane had destroyed all the photos she had left in the house out of anger. Shelby was too young to remember me and Kane helped with that by refusing to talk about me. That was the easy part." Alec stated this as if he had a secret that was beyond him just murdering his wife. Syon could see it just below the surface. Syon frowned.

Alec Campbell was much worse than anyone could have imagined.

Still focusing on his statement of murder, AC drew back as if he had been slapped. "You killed their mother? When? Why?"

Before Alec could reply, Syon rose from his chair and drew a hand over his closely cropped hair. Deep in his own thoughts, he took a gaited stance after planting himself in the far corner of the room. He didn't want to be anywhere near this man. They were dealing with a monster.

"I killed her shortly after Shelby was born. I told my mother and Alonso she ran off. That's when I gave my children to their grandmother."

AC tried to speak, but had to clear his throat to be heard. The disgust he felt was palpable. "Where is her body?"

Alec shook his head and sighed. "Never to be found I'm afraid. I threw her body in Belle River many years ago. It was never found so I'm assuming..." Instead of continuing he shrugged.

AC's thoughts were spinning. He was right Shelby and Kane's mother was long gone. After that many years, it was doubtful any remains could be found.

Syon spoke up. "This is all enlightening, and I suspect you have much more to tell, but I just have one more question then I'm out of here. You can finish up the rest of...of this with AC and I'll read about it in the papers." Syon rigidly gestured with a hand while trying to cope with his own repulsion of everything he'd just heard. He couldn't stay in the room much longer with this diabolical monster. He would get his answer and leave.

"Were you behind the accidents involving Queen?"

Alec answered without hesitation. "Yes. The first one was Santiago though. After he dipped on me, I had to handle the second one myself." That's all Syon needed to know, anything else was AC's problem. He knocked on the door to be released from this man's presence. He had consumed more than what he came for.

After Syon left, Alec Campbell, told AC everything he needed to know and then asked to be placed back in his cell, where AC obliged. Once they were done, AC had a pounding headache. He too had his fill of this man. In all of his career, he had never encounter anyone close to Alec Campbell, aka Davis Kane.

And just as predicted, the news media was ravenous over Alec's added crimes. So taken by what he had done, the media had dubbed him Killer Kane. Not only had he murdered his wife and son, he had also murdered Maureen Willis, Queen's mother. It was just good fortune that his mother had passed of natural causes before she too would have been deemed worthy of his annihilation. He had managed to eliminate everyone who could positively identify him as Davis Kane; all except for Queen.

Davis Kane's plan to disappear from the world started the day he left home for college. Despite his mother's adulation and devotion to her son, Davis hated his parents. His father was career military; moving his family all around the world. When they landed in Metro City, Davis' senior year of high school, he was finally to be free of roaming the earth. And after going off to college he was free of his parents. The last and only time he saw his mother after leaving was when he dropped his kids off for her to take care of. Elsa had been so overjoyed to see him again she never asked about the surgery or where he had been all those years. His father had died years earlier leaving her longing to see her son again. She was so overjoyed she planned a welcome home dinner just for him. Playing into that, Alec had offered to shop for the feast. He simply got into his car and kept driving; leaving his young children behind. Elsa never saw her son again.

During his course as an attorney is when he met Craven Wallace, who convinced him to invest in his ventures as an equal partner. Davis agreed only if his involvement was a silent one to which the former mayor was all too happy to oblige. Wallace needed the others to believe he was running the entire operation in order to maintain complete control. And after they were caught, instead of turning on Davis after he was convicted, Wallace saw an opportunity to continue their criminal enterprise, with his main goal to be quietly and illegally released from prison, when Davis became mayor. The planning for this involved 'Alec Campbell' tying up loose ends that could sink his chance in becoming top dog in Metro City, which lead to Kane's death and the attempt on Queen's life.

Davis never explained why he killed his common-law wife and mother of his children, but he did tell AC the reason Maureen Willis had to die. He was angry because she refused to become involved with him again after leaving her to begin his quest for money and power. She was his safe bet because she only knew him as Alec Campbell.

As more details were discovered of the city's now unseated mayor elect, the media was in information overload. Alec Campbell was a psychotic serial murderer who had fooled everyone, especially his supporters. Once the federal government learned of his ties to Craven Wallace's criminal activity in prison, Wallace and his followers were effectively shut down and spread across the country to separation facilities. Metro City breathed a sigh of relief. Its citizens were finally going to receive the city they deserved.

Chapter 32

Queen and Shelby sat staring at one another. They were sisters. The more the women looked into the face of other the other, they saw the resemblance. Syon was amazed that he hadn't seen it before. Looking at the two women together it was obvious they were related.

When he told Queen that she was indeed Alec's daughter and all of the terrible things he'd done, including killing her mother, she was stunned then angry. Angry he had taken her mother from her. Angry he had taken their child away. After the anger subsided, grief settled in. Her mother and unborn child had been murdered by a father she never knew. It had taken her weeks to gather enough courage to accept Shelby's invitation to meet. Queen didn't know if she could handle it. So much had happened to her. But once she realized she wasn't the only one hurting, she invited Shelby to dinner. Shelby too had lost a mother and a brother at the hands of their father. The two sisters had more in common than not.

The meeting was awkward at first. Shelby was grateful for Jon's presence. She didn't know what to say to her new sister. But after a while and a couple of glasses of wine, the two sisters cried together. Each mourning their loss. But after the tears of sadness came the tears of joy. They had each other now.

"Can you believe this man?" This was from Jon. He and Syon had taken their drinks to the terrace; letting the sisters have some alone time.

Syon shook his head. "I'm still expecting to wake up to find this all to be a dream."

"That asshole took so much from so many people. I wonder if any of his victims will be the same." Jon took a sip from his glass.

Syon grunted. "I doubt it. That monster took a child from us. Even though we can have more…" Syon let the sentence hang. Sure they could try again, but it wouldn't be the same. They would never get to hold their first child.

"Hey man, I'm sorry. I'd forgotten you two lost a child. There is just tragedy after tragedy with Alec or Davis or whoever the hell he is. This is one time I wish this state offered the death penalty."

"Amen to that." Syon lifted his glass in salute to the suggestion.

"I guess one good thing did come out of all of this. The sisters are together," Jon stated.

Syon swallowed. "Uh, huh, and don't forget Jess Ashford got her job back." He chuckled at the irony. The man did everything to destroy Jess only for her to be the one to completely annihilate him. Karma was truly just.

After Metro City's latest and possibly greatest scandal, the city's interim DA quietly resigned and moved out of the country, wanting nothing more to do with the tainted city. He felt the city's depraved run with its top officials would ruin any possible future goals he may have. The city's citizens who were quick to condemn Jess

Ashford found themselves in a forgiving mood after their misguided trust of their former mayor-elect. At least they knew all of Jess's sins. They found that Jess Ashford's escapades paled in comparison to what Campbell brought down on them, not to mention she was the one to bring him down. The city officials begged her to take her old job back with most of the city in agreement. They needed her tough as nails agenda to get things done and clean up their fair city.

"Jon chuckled." The woman is hell on wheels if anything else.

Read other novels written by Katrina Avant.

Amazon.com

Barnes&Noble.com

Follow her on Instagram * Facebook * YouTube

∞

Katrina also writes under her alter-ego Olivia M. Dutton. Check out her great reads!

Olivia's Novels

www.ingramcontent.com/pod-product-compliance
Lightning Source LLC
Chambersburg PA
CBHW072104170626
46813CB00004B/1454